"Any sign of them?"

Bethany didn't answer, and Daniel glanced in her direction. She was as white as a sheet and had pressed herself as close as possible to the truck door.

He laughed. He couldn't help himself. The look on her face was just too comical to ignore. "Are you okay?"

She shook her head. "No. You're wild!" The tone of her voice made it perfectly clear what she thought of his driving.

"What?" He raised an eyebrow, giving her his best innocent look.

"Remind me to never let you drive anywhere ever again," she said under her breath. "I think I'm going to throw up all over your nice floor mats."

"Come on. I'm a good driver," he said with a smile.

She narrowed her eyes. "At least tell me you lost our tail."

"Yep."

"Then it was worth it." She moaned. "I guess," she qualified.

Daniel pulled up behind the storefront and killed the engine, then turned to Bethany. "Okay. Are you ready for this?"

Bethany grimaced. "Ready as I'll ever be."

Kathleen Tailer is a senior attorney II who works for the Supreme Court of Florida in the office of the state courts administrator. She graduated from Florida State University College of Law after earning her BA from the University of New Mexico. She and her husband have eight children, five of whom they adopted from the state of Florida. She enjoys photography and playing drums on the worship team at Calvary Chapel, Thomasville, Georgia.

Books by Kathleen Tailer

Love Inspired Suspense

Under the Marshal's Protection
The Reluctant Witness
Perilous Refuge
Quest for Justice
Undercover Jeopardy

UNDERCOVER JEOPARDY

KATHLEEN TAILER

HARLEQUIN® LOVE INSPIRED® SUSPENSE

Recycling programs
for this product may
not exist in your area.

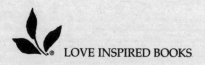

LOVE INSPIRED BOOKS

ISBN-13: 978-1-335-23205-2

Undercover Jeopardy

Copyright © 2019 by Kathleen Tailer

www.Harlequin.com

Printed in U.S.A.

And we know that all things work together for good to them that love God, to them who are the called according to his purpose.... If God be for us, who can be against us?
—*Romans* 8:28-31

For all the missionaries around the world who have dedicated their lives to sharing the love of Jesus Christ, including Beverly and Greg Wootton, Isaac and Clea Wootton and their wonderful children, and Connie Rose. May God continue to bless you as you do His work across the African continent and beyond.

ONE

Detective Daniel Morley wrote the date on his deposit slip, then double-checked it against the large calendar the bank had posted on one of the columns near the customer service desk among the green pine trim and the red-and-white candy cane decorations. December 14. It had been one year since Bethany Walker had disappeared from his life. An entire year of searching and coming up empty. He was a detective—one of the best in the business, but he'd utterly failed to find her, despite his herculean efforts. She had been his fiancée but now, instead of celebrating their wedding anniversary, he was solemnly remembering the last time he'd seen her and the hurtful words he'd spoken during their argument right before she'd driven away. He should have gone after her. Now, he didn't know if he'd ever even see her again, and the calendar before him was just one more reminder of how long she had been missing from his life.

People didn't just disappear, and yet, Bethany seemed to have done just that. Her apartment lease had been paid in advance, but despite several evenings of surveillance, he had not seen a single person enter or leave. He'd even used his law enforcement credentials to complete a welfare check. Daniel and the landlord walked through the rooms together, but there was no sign of Bethany, or any clues as to her whereabouts. Her refrigerator was bare, and there were only a few staples left in the pantry. It was obvious that she wasn't living there. But then where was she staying? And if she'd moved and left the Chattanooga area completely, why had she kept the lease? It was a mystery.

"Excuse me, can I please have one of those?" An older lady smiled at him as her voice brought him out of his reverie. She motioned toward the stack of deposit slips sitting in front of him, and he smiled back at her as he pushed them in her direction so they were within her reach.

"Of course. Here you go."

The bullets from a semi-automatic machine gun slammed into the ceiling, quickly covering Daniel with dust and debris from the tiles overhead as the noise shattered the peaceful Friday morning. He instinctively crouched, taking the older woman with him and pushing her under the desk for safety. He pulled out his service 9 mm pistol, his eyes darting around the room as he assessed the situation.

"Everyone get down on the floor!" The voice was masculine and accentuated by more gunfire. Several of the customers screamed, and the fear in the room was palpable and made the air feel heavy and thick. A man in a black hoodie and jeans jumped up on the counter and started waving his rifle around. He let loose with another stream of bullets into the ceiling.

"Quiet, now! The next person who makes a noise dies!" he yelled.

The room was instantly silent, and all eyes were on the robber, awaiting his next command. The man's face was covered by a mask that distorted his features, and he paced back and forth like a caged tiger. The mask gave away the fact that he was Caucasian and little else, and there was a grotesque smile on it that made his expression seem malevolent and evil.

The robber swung his gun toward a woman teller in a gray suit who already had tears streaming down her cheeks. She was trembling and seemed almost frozen in place. The color seemed to drain from her face once she realized the robber had focused his attention on her. "Get your hand away from the counter!" he yelled, as he fired a barrage of bullets over her head. "If you touch that silent alarm button, you're dead." She ducked and dropped to the floor, her body still shaking uncontrollably.

He turned back to the crowd in the lobby and immediately fired a burst toward the ceiling again. "Okay, everyone. You have five seconds to get down on the floor. Anybody still standing after five seconds will be shot. Understand? One, two…"

Daniel scanned the room. From his vantage point where he was still partially concealed by the table, he could see three other robbers. They were all wearing the same black hoodies and jeans. They even had the same masks with identical evil smiles, just like the one worn by their leader. One large muscular robber had positioned himself near the bank's front door and had put a metal cable around the handles, effectively locking the doors and everyone inside the building while also keeping others out. This man was taller than the others and looked like he either worked out on a regular basis or, at a minimum, played a sport that kept him in excellent shape. He had disarmed the guard who had been stationed by the front door, and was motioning to him and two other men to join the rest of the hostages in the lobby of the bank.

The other two robbers were both skinnier than the man by the front door and younger, if Daniel was any judge of the way they held themselves. Maybe they were in their twenties? Their movements seemed reckless and exceedingly hyper, or they could have just been high on the adrenaline rush that came from shooting up a bank and scaring innocent people. Either way, it was obvious that they were extremely dangerous and volatile. One of the robbers approached the customers who were slower to obey, and he tossed his gun back and forth between his hands, yelling at them and forcing them into compliance. He seemed to have some sort of facial hair under his mask, and Daniel nicknamed him Hairy in his mind. The other robber followed closely behind Hairy at first, but then finally moved away and started spraying paint over the security cameras that were set in three corners of the room. Once the cameras were disabled, he tossed the spray can aside and stationed himself near a doorway that appeared to lead back to the public bathrooms. Daniel noticed he had a small limp and tended to drag his right foot a bit.

"We're not here for you," the leader yelled over the confusion, still pacing from his perch on the countertop. "We just want to make a small withdrawal." He made a point of making eye contact with any of the hostages who dared to look in his direction. "No one will get hurt as long as you do everything we say."

Daniel looked to the left and saw two men, both crawling away from the front counter area and heading toward the back of the bank where the desks and offices were found. One was wearing a suit and appeared to be a bank employee. The other was wearing shorts and a button-down shirt and seemed to be following the other one. It was apparent that both were looking for a safe place to hide. They didn't escape the notice of the lead robber, however, who jumped down, ran so that he was directly in front of them and pointed his gun straight at their heads. "Put your faces on the floor. Both of you. Now!"

Daniel moved so he could get a better look at the leader but still be shielded by the counter. So far, he had escaped the robbers' notice, but he knew it couldn't last much longer. He raised his gun, taking aim at the man's chest. One quick shot was all it would take to stop the leader in his tracks and foil this robbery attempt here and now. He might even save the two men on the floor in the process. His finger flexed on the trigger.

"Freeze." The cold metal of the barrel pushed against his skull. He tried to turn a bit to see who was behind him, but the pressure increased against his head and he stopped. He hadn't realized there was a fifth robber. He mentally kicked himself for missing that important fact. His inconceivable mistake might just have cost him his life.

"Hands up. Now."

The voice sounded familiar to him, but he couldn't place it. He guessed that the robber was a woman by the tone of her voice, even though she was obviously trying to disguise the sound by making it gritty and deeper. He slowly raised his hands as she leaned forward and grabbed his pistol, then pushed him from behind. "Get over there by the wall, hero."

He chanced a look behind him but only got a quick glance before she pushed him again. It was enough of a look to get a basic impression of the robber, but little else. All he could tell was that she was definitely a woman. Her stature was lean but still feminine, despite the baggy jeans and hoodie she was wearing, and she was quite a bit shorter than the other robbers. Even with the mask that disguised her features, he'd also gotten a good enough look to tell that the eyes and lips were quite ladylike.

"Against the wall, everyone," the leader yelled. The robbers continued motioning with their guns and herding the customers and bank staff toward the far wall until the whole group was lined up against it. Daniel watched the process as the woman robber marched him over to join the rest of the hostages. So far, he counted eighteen of them, including both customers and bank employees. He saw the old lady that had been near him when the robbers had entered the bank, and her eyes were large and wet beneath her glasses. Her skin had paled, and her weathered hands desperately gripped her large black pocketbook that she held close to her chest. She was obviously terrified. He glanced at the others. There were seven other women and ten men, including himself. He kept his hands up as he walked to the group of frightened people, but when he took his place at the end of the line, he didn't sit like the others. Instead, he turned and kept his hands raised in mock surrender and took a step toward the woman robber. When he spoke, he kept his tone low and calm.

"You don't have to do this. Nobody's been hurt. You can turn around and walk away now before this goes any further."

"Just shut up and do as you're told," she responded, her voice cold.

"Think about what you're doing," Daniel implored softly, still trying to sound as non-threatening as possible.

"I can assure you that we've given this a great deal of thought. Now have a seat." She gestured with her gun and Daniel acknowledged her but didn't sit. He could see the bulge of the weapon that she had taken from him and stuffed into the waistband of her jeans. No cop wanted his service pistol to end up in the hands of a criminal, and Daniel was no exception. He made a vow to recover that gun before this episode was over. Funny—she hadn't asked why he had been carrying a gun. Tennessee did have very liberal concealed weapon permit laws, but still…

He pushed that thought aside and decided to try talking to her one more time. "The laws have gotten tougher," he said quietly. "Bank robbery is federal. You could get a life sentence. The minimum is twenty-five years when guns are involved. If you give up now—"

"Not happening," she said roughly, aiming her gun directly at his midriff. "Don't be a hero. Sit down with the others." Her voice was low but threatening.

"Is this guy giving you a problem?" Daniel turned and saw one of the younger robbers coming toward him. He thought it was Hairy, the one who had been tossing the gun around, but he couldn't be sure. The criminal's stance was aggressive as he approached, and Daniel braced for the battle that was heading his way.

"It's under control," she snarled.

"Doesn't look like it's under control to me." He lifted his rifle as if to hit Daniel in the face, but before he could do anything further, the woman stepped in front of Daniel, her stance protective.

"Back off," the woman exclaimed angrily. "I said I have it under control."

The young man paused a moment, his body moving from foot to foot as if he was filled with energy and was about to explode. "Sure you do."

She took a step closer to the other robber, her voice tight. "The deal was nobody gets hurt. Now stay out of my way, J.P.," she growled.

He leaned closer and his whisper was a low hiss. "No names, remember?"

She motioned around her. "Who's gonna hear me? I'm serious. Stay out of my way."

"You stay out of *my* way, girl. I didn't want you here in the first place." He spun around and angrily threatened one of the other customers with his rifle.

"Get back, did you hear me?" He raised the weapon up as if he was going to hit someone else, then abruptly stalked off.

Bethany blew out a breath of relief as the man moved away. Her heart was beating so strongly she was sure J.P. could hear it. What in the world was Daniel doing here, of all places? Thankfully, she had been able to distract J.P. before any further violence had happened. She had once seen J.P. beat a man into unconsciousness for borrowing his truck without asking. He was vengeful and a loose cannon, and there was no telling how far he would go if he continued unchecked. She said a small prayer of thanks under her breath, then motioned to Daniel with her gun.

"Sit with the others. Now."

Daniel put his hands up in a motion of mock surrender, then nodded and sat. She didn't like the way he was studying her, but it couldn't be helped.

She glanced over at J.P., who was stalking the floor, threatening anyone who dared to look up. The kid was a hothead, and she had been trying to avoid him ever since she'd infiltrated this band for the FBI a year ago. He was always challenging her, and if anyone was going to blow her cover, it would probably be him.

She looked down at Daniel and her heart continued to pound. She didn't think he had recognized her, and she wondered how long she could keep her identity a secret from him if this robbery took longer than expected. Her feelings were in a jumbled mess where Daniel was concerned. She had loved him once, or thought she had, but that seemed like a lifetime ago. Their last words had been said in anger, and she had taken this undercover assignment only a few days later. It had been an excellent escape and helped her refocus her energy after their breakup. Now that a year had passed, she had no desire to bring those feelings to the surface and sort through them all over again. The past was better left in the past.

"Okay, I want everyone's cell phones. Now!" She turned to see their leader, Jackson, swinging his gun around and carrying a trash can. He walked down the line of hostages and waited impatiently as they each deposited their cell phones in the metal can. The captives were all in different stages between panic and disbelief. A couple of the women were crying, and a few of the men were pale and withdrawn, but they all complied with Jackson's orders. When he came to Daniel, he stopped and Bethany held her breath, hoping that neither Jackson nor Daniel would start an altercation. Being undercover meant sometimes walking a thin line between the legal and illegal. Her participation in this bank robbery had been authorized by her handler at the FBI, so they could trace the stolen money and make bigger arrests, but it was hard to see anyone get hurt. Still, she would blow her cover in a heartbeat if any of the robbers tried to kill an innocent victim. The problem was that she knew Daniel was a fellow officer who would do everything within his power to foil this robbery. She held her breath, not sure what to expect, her body tense and ready to react.

"Was this man giving you trouble?" Jackson asked, looking between Daniel and the other robbers.

A cold sweat ran down her back. Should she tell their leader that Daniel was a cop? Her mind focused on the heaviness of Daniel's weapon resting in the waistband of her jeans. If he saw Daniel's police badge or somehow discovered that she'd known he was law enforcement and hadn't said anything, it could blow her cover. But if she did tell, Jackson might lose his temper and try to hurt Daniel, and she would be forced to intervene. There was no telling what he would do if he found out one of the hostages was a detective with the local police department. This entire assignment could blow up in the next few moments if she didn't quickly think of a solution. Her mind was spinning when surprisingly J.P. solved her problem for her.

"He was mouthing off. I had to show him who was in charge," J.P. offered with a sardonic grin.

Bethany blew out a breath of relief, her dilemma temporarily fixed. She watched Jackson carefully, waiting for his reaction.

Jackson finally nodded, apparently accepting the response, and pointed his gun at Daniel's head. "Give me your cell phone."

Daniel's pulled out his cell phone that was clipped to his belt and in the same motion, surreptitiously pushed his detective shield into his pocket, hiding it from view. Bethany noticed and quickly looked down so it seemed like she wasn't paying attention. He dropped the phone in the trash can with the others and Jackson continued down the line, none the wiser.

Suddenly a shot rang out, and J.P. shrieked and grabbed his side. A dark circle of blood appeared on the hoodie near J.P.'s abdomen, and J.P. slowly sank to the floor, his face contorted with pain. Bethany crouched, her weapon ready, searching the room for the source of the shot. Would the next bullet take her out?

TWO

Bethany turned just in time to see a security guard slip back behind a corner in the hallway leading to the back of the building. She fired back, but made sure her shots were high. Good grief! Hadn't Jackson cleared the building? She noticed Jackson motioning to Terrell, the big, well-built robber who had locked the front doors and was closer to the guard's hiding place than any of the other robbers. They had all studied the floor plans of the bank before the theft, and they all knew that if Terrell was careful, he could sneak up on the guard from behind and disarm him by going through a second hallway that was accessible from behind the tellers' counter. Terrell nodded to Jackson and silently disappeared through the door. Bethany hoped Terrell would be reasonable and not hurt the guard. He was a true believer in the cause, but he wasn't by nature a violent person. A few minutes later, they heard some shouting from the hallway, and Terrell led the security guard out with his hands up and forced him to join the line of hostages. He had been disarmed and had a recalcitrant expression on his face, but he didn't look injured. Bethany was instantly relieved. Her biggest dread in participating in this crime was that someone innocent would get hurt or killed. It was bad enough that J.P. got shot. She surely didn't want any other casualties.

"Trying to be a hero?" Jackson sneered when the guard and Terrell reached the group. The guard didn't answer, and Bethany glanced at her watch. Things were going downhill, fast. They needed to get into the vault, get what they came for and get out of here. This whole robbery was taking way too long. A wave of anxiety washed over her as she watched Jackson motion to the guard with his gun. "Sit down with the others." The guard complied, warily eyeing J.P., who was still laying on the floor, bleeding and moaning loudly and intermittently. He was right to be worried. If J.P. weren't hurt so badly, he surely would have been so angry about being shot that he would have killed the guard outright just for revenge. J.P. had always been the one wild card in the whole operation. It was almost a blessing that he was out of the mix and wouldn't be able to hurt anybody. Still, she didn't want him to die.

As Jackson gave orders for Terrell to sweep the place and make sure no one else was hiding in the back, Bethany went over to J.P.'s side. She put her rifle down and pulled up J.P.'s shirt so she could examine his wound. The fabric was already soaked with blood. He grabbed her arm and squeezed her hard. "I can't believe he shot me. Help me, Hailey. He wasn't supposed to shoot me."

Bethany nodded and met his eye, trying to reassure him. "Sure thing, J.P. Just let me take a look." Hailey was her undercover name, yet it still sounded odd to her ears. She thought she'd eventually get used to it, especially since she'd been undercover for a year with this group.

She examined the wound carefully, then gingerly rolled him to his side so she could see if the bullet had gone out his back. Thankfully, she found an exit wound. Even though it was bleeding profusely, she thought it was merely a flesh wound. If she could just stop the blood flow, he should be back to his normal nasty self in only a few weeks. She carefully pulled off her hoodie, found some scissors in a drawer in a nearby worker's desk and cut the sweatshirt into strips, thankful for the latex gloves that the robbers were all wearing that kept her hands free of the blood. She kept her mask in place and still had on the black T-shirt she had been wearing underneath the hoodie, but now it was clear to everyone that she was a woman. There was no way to hide her body shape or her dark blond hair that was pulled back in a slick ponytail. She made a bandage out of the fabric and applied pressure for a few minutes before wrapping the rest of the strips around him to securely hold the bandage in place. Once she finished dressing his wound, she tied a knot and leaned over him.

"Alright, J.P.," she whispered for his ears only. "You lie still, okay?" She put his hands on top of the knot. "Hold that bandage right there as tightly as you can to stop the bleeding. Got it?" She squeezed his arm. *God, please save his life and change his heart.*

She grabbed her rifle again and stood. At least now J.P. had a fighting chance. She glanced nonchalantly in Daniel's direction, but a sliver of fear slid down her spine when she saw the look on his face. His eyes were burning into her like hot coals. It was obvious that he had recognized her, and anger and frustration radiated from his head to his toes. Now that he knew who she was, would he blow her cover? She met his eyes, which were following her every movement. Maybe it wasn't anger she saw there but confusion and hurt instead. She looked away, not ready to confront Daniel or the emotions that caused a tightening in her chest.

Bethany Walker, his ex-fiancée, stood not twenty feet from him. Daniel still couldn't believe it. But what was she doing robbing banks? He sat up a little straighter and watched her carefully as she tended to the other robber. He wanted to march right over to her and demand an explanation, but something inside of him urged caution. Bethany was a top special agent for the FBI. She had to be on assignment. Still, law enforcement was in the business of preventing crime, not creating crime, so why was she involved in an illegal activity like bank robbery? In Daniel's book, Bethany's actions violated the oath of a law enforcement officer. How could she protect and serve if she was the one wielding the rifle?

Daniel's attention was quickly diverted as the leader abruptly shot another stream of bullets into the ceiling. "Alright, who is the manager here?" He paced in front of the terrified group of hostages. All of the other robbers besides Hairy, wait, what had Bethany called him? Oh, yeah, J.P. All of the robbers besides J.P. stood behind the leader, keeping a wary eye on the situation, their guns at the ready. J.P. lay moaning on the floor right where he had fallen. The leader moved closer to one of the men who obviously worked at the bank. "Are you the manager?"

The man put his hands up in mock surrender and shook his head. "No, no, it's that guy." He pointed to an older man in a dark suit who gave him a withering look.

The leader smiled and sauntered over to the manager. He motioned with his gun. "Get up, mister manager. I'd like to see the inside of your vault."

"It's time locked," the man sputtered.

"You're quite right," the leader said with a smile as he checked his watch. "Isn't it wonderful that we're here at precisely the correct time? Now, if you'll just come punch your code into the keypad, we'll be in business."

Daniel could tell the man was terrified but was also trying his best to stall and protect the bank. His hesitance wasn't lost on the leader either, who grabbed the manager's tie and brought him to his feet. Then he pushed him toward the back of the bank where the vault was located. The man stumbled but righted himself and started walking. The leader, the robber with the limp and the bodybuilder robber all followed him, each carrying a large black duffel bag they had brought in with them when they'd first entered the bank. Daniel noticed there were two other bags of supplies the robbers had carried in, and he wondered briefly what was inside of them. He remembered that bank robberies usually averaged six minutes from start to finish, and he wondered fleetingly when this team was planning to make their escape. They had already been in the bank quite a long time by robbery standards and had gone way past the average.

Bethany was the only robber left to watch the hostages, although J.P. was still lying on the floor, suffering from his injuries. She took over the pacing in front of the line of people, and Daniel watched her carefully, wondering if there was any way he could find an opportunity to talk to her in private so he could figure out what was going on.

The phone suddenly rang, the shrill sound startling the group. Bethany ignored it, but after the tenth ring or so, Daniel spoke up. "Want me to answer that for you?"

"Stay where you are," she said flatly, pointing her gun at him. Now that he knew her identity, Daniel knew he wasn't in danger and she wouldn't fire, but he didn't want to push her too far and ruin her cover either. Still, he had big questions for her. How could he get her alone to talk? Was it even possible in the confines of this insane robbery situation?

The ringing continued.

"Look, you must know this is taking too long. The police are probably already outside surrounding the place. They're undoubtedly controlling the phones, and that's a negotiator calling to talk you through this mess. You need to listen to him." A couple of the other hostages groaned when he spoke, apparently frustrated with his goading.

"Shut up," Bethany said roughly, taking a step in his direction. "It's too early for the police to be here."

The ringing continued.

Daniel couldn't help himself. All of the hurt and frustration he'd felt at losing Bethany suddenly came to a head, and now that he had found her, he had to push forward, regardless of the circumstances. "It's got to be them," he said, not knowing if it really was or not, but trying hard to sell the bluff. He started to stand and confront her, but she moved in closer and actually pointed the gun directly at his head. When she spoke, her voice was low and cold like ice. "I said, stay where you are. Don't move again unless you want a new hole in your head."

He looked up into her eyes, those gray-blue eyes that reminded him of polished steel, and backed off. There was strength there, and memories flooded back at him. He remembered her laughing during a funny part of a movie and accepting his comfort when her cat died. They had shared a lot during their relationship, but the woman standing in front of him brandishing the gun as part of a robbery gang seemed like a total stranger. Yet, the love remained. He couldn't erase it, no matter how much he had tried to forget her during the last year. He eyed her critically, noticing small details about her. She was thinner now, and her hair was a bit longer, but now that he knew her identity, it was hard to figure out why he hadn't identified her sooner, even with the mask distorting her facial features.

Why? Why had she left him without an explanation? Had she never loved him in the first place? Why had she never followed through and walked down the aisle with him? Where had she been for the last year? Pain slashed across his chest, but he tried his best to push those questions out of his mind. As much as he wanted to confront her and demand answers, they would have to wait. This wasn't the time or place. In fact, he might never get a chance to talk to Bethany privately during this bank robbery. Right now, he needed to focus on stopping this crime, if it was possible, and make sure nobody got hurt, including the woman he loved.

Suddenly, another man from the middle of the group started to stand, as well. Bethany swung her rifle in his direction and let fly a short burst of bullets. She must have aimed high on purpose, because each shot missed and hit the wood paneling about two feet above his head. Still, the shots had the desired effect, and the man quickly sat back down again, his eyes wide with fear. She took a few steps back, apparently making sure she had a good view of all the hostages.

When she spoke, her voice was tough as nails, and her body language said she was more than just angry. "I said, stay where you are, all of you. Make no mistake, I am in control of this room and I missed on purpose. The next person that moves will be dead. Got it? I don't have to miss. I'm an excellent shot. We'll be out of here in just a few more minutes, and then you can all go back to your lives. Until then, you stay quiet and out of our way."

Daniel couldn't keep silent despite her orders. He

changed his tactic, knowing Bethany would always want to make sure a life wasn't lost during an operation but also ensuring he didn't make her appear vulnerable in front of the other hostages. The last thing he needed was for the hostages to feel empowered and attempt to rush her or try to take away her weapon. "We get it. You're in charge. But please, let someone take your man outside. He's injured and needs medical attention." Daniel paused, waiting to see how Bethany would respond to his argument. Seeing no change in her expression, he tried a different approach. "If he dies, it will go worse for you in the long run." Daniel knew she had a better chance of keeping her cover intact if no one died during this operation, and if law enforcement could interrogate the robber lying on the floor, all the better.

She laughed. She actually laughed at his suggestion. "So the police can arrest him on sight? No, thank you."

Was she being sincere, or acting the part? He honestly couldn't tell. Maybe he didn't know her anymore after all. A lot could change in a year. "He'll die if he doesn't get help. He'll also slow down your escape." He pointed to one of the stronger looking men. "Let him do it. He can carry the guy out and make sure he gets the help he needs."

He waited as the seconds slowly ticked by, stretching into minutes. The air felt thick.

THREE

As if on cue, the phone started ringing again, slicing into the silence. Bethany eyed her watch, then the doorway that led to the vault. Something must have gone wrong; they were taking way too long to get the money and emerge from the back room where the vault was located. She knew that Jackson had already knocked out the video feeds and alarm system, but she wondered fleetingly if there was an issue with the bank manager's code. Jackson swore he could bypass the electronic lock on the vault by doing some fancy wiring if he had to, but she wasn't as confident in his abilities as he was. If he wasn't going to be able to open it after all, her undercover mission was going to last even longer than she'd thought. The group she had infiltrated needed money to operate, and if they didn't get it here and now, they would have to commit more crimes in the future to fund their operation. It was better all-around if they were successful here today. Then she could focus on building her case and making her arrests as the robbers put their more devious plans into motion.

She eyed the group of hostages in front of her and tried to look tough and demanding. So far, she was confident that they wouldn't do anything foolish—except for Daniel, that is. She could tell he was testing her. Maybe if their relationship hadn't ended so badly he wouldn't be challenging her, but now he knew her true identity, and she wasn't sure what to expect. No matter what, she couldn't blow her cover. Not here and now when she had come so far and given this operation a year of her life.

"Let me get that phone for you," Daniel suggested again. She swung back and stalked toward him. She doubted that the ringing phone was the police. This was a place of business after all, and phones probably rang constantly throughout the day. Still, the sound was eerily annoying, but not as annoying as the look of hurt in Daniel's eyes that he was apparently unable to hide. His expression surprised her. Hadn't they both said angry words to each other on that fateful day when they had ended their relationship? Pride made her push past the feelings that were starting to bubble in her chest.

Maybe she had hurt him by not giving him an opportunity to explain after the big blowup. He never apologized, but she had basically vanished and never given him a chance to do so. She paused, reliving some of the argument in her mind. She was mature enough to realize that the fault had been hers, as well. Her disappearance had been swift after their relationship had collapsed, but her superiors had required an immediate response when they had offered her this assignment, and there had been no time to contact anyone. She had jumped at the opportunity to go undercover and further her career, but it had also been an excellent way to avoid the hurt and anger she had felt and evade any further confrontation. She had never thought of herself as a coward, but she had definitely wanted to avoid ever running into Daniel again. She glanced at him now and another wave of emotion swept over her. Why did he have to be here today? He was already pushing her buttons. Why wouldn't he just sit down and stay out of her way?

Terrell suddenly emerged from the back room, which instantly stopped her woolgathering and made her alert. His hands were empty except for the rifle, and he approached Bethany and leaned forward so only she could hear. "Jackson is having trouble with the safe. The manager couldn't get his code to work, so Jackson is working on the wiring. He's trying to override the system."

"We don't have time for this," she hissed. "The cops will be here in no time."

"Jackson wants to wait. He's convinced he can open it if he's just given a few more minutes."

"J.P. might die."

Terrell laughed. "I never liked him anyway, and I sure never thought you'd care with the way he treats you."

"I've never liked him either," she whispered back. "But that doesn't mean I want him to die." She glanced around at the people lined against the counter, then at her watch. "We really need to get out of here. Forget the vault. Let's get the cash out of the registers and bounce." Fear swept down her spine. She wasn't afraid of getting caught. Her FBI handler would deal with that if she were arrested. But the longer this robbery stretched out, the more probable it became that someone would get hurt.

As if to accent the point, the phone started ringing again.

Terrell motioned toward the phone. "Go ahead and answer it. I'll keep an eye on these folks. If it's the cops, we need to start the dialogue so they don't raid the place."

She hesitated but finally slung her rifle over her back and walked over to where the phone was ringing on the desk. She picked it up. "What?"

"This is Sergeant Michaels with the police department. Who am I talking to?"

"You can call me Bonnie." Bethany smiled, thinking of Bonnie and Clyde. "By the way, you get an A+ for response time. I must say, you got here quicker than we expected."

"We aim to serve," he responded dryly. "Am I speaking to the one in charge?"

"Not likely."

"Well, who would that be?"

"He's a bit busy right now. We'll have to hold introductions later."

Sergeant Michaels paused, obviously taking notes. "Alright, Bonnie. Is anybody hurt in there?"

"We've had a few mishaps."

"Do you want to let me send in some emergency techs to take care of them?"

"No, Sergeant, I don't think that would be a good idea. In case you haven't noticed, we've strapped some C-4 on the doors. It would get a bit exciting if you tried to get in here."

There was another pause. "We don't want anyone to get hurt here."

Bethany nodded, switching the phone from one ear to the other so she could keep a better eye on Terrell and the hostages. "We share that goal." She lowered her voice. "My boss, however, isn't as concerned about that as we are. I urge you not to try to breech the front or the back of the bank." There. She'd warned them. Her handler should have already notified the local authorities of her role in the heist and of what they were facing, but there were no guarantees. She had notified her handler of the details and he, in turn, had passed on the details, such as the explosives at the doors, to the local teams. Still, she knew she was in a risky position, and there was always a possibility that things could go terribly wrong. Since banks were federally insured, the FBI always got called in when a robbery occurred, but that didn't mean the communication between the various law enforcement agencies was decent or accurate.

Sergeant Michaels cleared his throat. "Can you give your boss a message for me?"

"Sure thing, Sergeant."

"Well, Bonnie, first let him know we've got control of the landlines coming out of the bank, so you can reach us by picking up any of the phones in the building. Anytime you or your boss want to talk, I'll be available."

"Aren't you the Southern gentleman?" She let a tad of sarcasm touch her voice. She was supposed to be a bank robber after all. Sergeant Michaels didn't take the bait though, and when he spoke again, his voice was calm and controlled.

"You should also know that we have this bank surrounded. You're not going to be able to get out of there without my help." He paused. "You believe that, don't you, Bonnie? That I'm here to help you?"

She laughed. "Sure. You'll help me all the way to a prison cell."

Again, he didn't react to her taunting. "I'm here to help make sure you don't get killed. I don't want any more bloodshed. Let's end this peacefully. I want you to be able to see tomorrow."

"Sergeant, let me remind you that we have eighteen hostages in here. If you want them all to walk out of here, you'll keep your distance. Otherwise, you'll be picking up the pieces."

"Well, Bonnie, like I said, my goal today is to make sure no one gets hurt. What can I do for you to make sure we resolve this quickly and quietly?"

"I'll get back to you on that." She hung up, not willing to drag out the conversation. She was sure they were recording her voice and doing a voice recognition test. Hopefully that would remind them that she was law enforcement and the snipers that would inevitably be put in place wouldn't put a target on her.

She glanced at her watch and noted the time. Jackson was taking way too long to get into that safe. They'd had a plan in place if the police showed up before they could escape, but it was dangerous. Now they had no choice but to start following it. She thought about J.P. lying on the floor and stole a glance in his direction. He was still grimacing and holding his side where he'd been shot, but he was moving around less. His face was also much paler, and she wondered if he was going into shock. She decided to check on him and went back over to his side. She bent and took a look under his bandages while Terrell checked in with Jackson at the vault. She kept a close eye on the hostages while she did so, but none of them seemed anxious to challenge her authority this time, even though she had to lay down her rifle to check J.P.'s wounds.

"How's it look?" J.P. asked, his voice laced with pain.

"Not so good," she said softly. She kept the panic out of her voice, but she was deeply concerned about the amount of blood on the bandages. Daniel was right. J.P. needed a doctor, and he needed one now. If he didn't get one, he might end up bleeding out right there on the floor. She adjusted the bandages and tied them a bit tighter. "Don't worry, J.P. I'm going to get you some help."

He grabbed her arm and held it way too tightly. "Don't turn me over to the cops," he hissed.

"I don't have a choice. If I don't, you'll die right here and right now. Is that what you want?"

"Don't do it, Hailey. I'm warning you."

"Warning me?" she laughed, even though there was

no mirth in her voice. "What do you plan to do to me if you're six feet under, pushing up daisies?"

He tried to pull himself up but groaned and fell back against the floor. He grabbed for her arm again, but she stayed just out of reach. "I'd rather die than get caught. If you turn me over to the cops, I'll end up in prison, and it will be all your fault. If that happens, I'll make you pay. I swear I will."

"Maybe," she said with a frown. "But at least you'll be alive." She knew J.P. was a true believer in the cause, and the chances of him ratting them out were next to nil once he was arrested, but she took his threat against her seriously. J.P. was a dangerous enemy to have. Still, she couldn't just let him die.

"How is he?" Terrell asked as he reappeared and sauntered over to her side. He must have noticed her worried expression because some of the confidence went out of his step as he looked between her and J.P.

"Not good." She stood and motioned toward the vault. "How's the progress back there?"

Terrell shrugged. "The same. Slow but steady."

She motioned to J.P. "He's going to die if we don't get him some help. He's bleeding way too much."

Terrell shook his head. "Then he dies. The boss won't like it if we let anybody in here or if we let them take him to a hospital. You know the rules."

J.P. called out to Terrell. "Hey, man. Don't let her turn me over to the cops."

Bethany moved so she was blocking Terrell's view of J.P. and caught the bigger man's eye. "Did you hear what I said? He'll die if we don't get him to a hospital."

"Then let him die," Terrell suddenly yelled, his voice filling with anger. "Aren't you listening? There's a bigger picture here, woman. You can't take a chance that he'll talk." He stalked up to Bethany and leaned over her, his stance threatening. "The cause is the only thing that matters."

She didn't back down. "I won't let him die."

"It's not up to you. Listen to what he's saying. He doesn't even want your help."

"Do you want his death on your conscience?" she spat. She knew Terrell was twice her size and strength, but she had to stand up to him. This was important. This was life and death. She looked into his eyes and wondered how far he would go. He looked angry enough to shoot her just for daring to challenge him. Or would he shoot J.P. himself and make the whole argument moot? Despite his glare, she couldn't back down. "I don't want him on my conscience when I know I could have saved him."

"The boss will not be happy about it. Let him die."

Bethany looked from J.P. to Terrell, both of whom were glowering. Her insides were fighting a raging battle. Was this the end of her undercover assignment right here and now? Even if it meant she had wasted a year of her life on this mission, life was too precious to just throw it away.

"I'm sorry, boys. I can't just stand here and do nothing. I won't."

Terrell nodded. "Okay. You've made your choice."

He raised his weapon.

FOUR

Daniel watched the confrontation and felt his adrenaline surge as his protective instincts kicked in. Even if it cost him his life, he would not stand by and watch Bethany get hurt. He didn't know if the bodybuilder robber would actually shoot her or not, but he couldn't wait and find out. Daniel didn't like the way the man was holding his rifle. He stood and moved toward them. "Hey now."

In one fleeting second, all of the bigger man's anger focused on Daniel. He took several steps toward him and raised the butt of his weapon as if preparing to hit Daniel across the face. "You stay back, do you hear me?"

Daniel put his hands up and retreated a few steps. He had accomplished his objective—he had distracted him and gotten him to move away from Bethany. "Yeah, I hear you."

The bodybuilder loomed threateningly over him, and Daniel could see the red in his eyes and smell garlic on his breath even through the mask. "Sit back down! Now! Or I'll make sure you never stand up again!"

Daniel obeyed, his hands still up in front of him. He didn't know what to expect and wouldn't have been surprised if the robber had bashed him with the rifle just for good measure. The man was so angry his hands were shaking. It had to be the stress. This heist was taking longer than any of them had probably expected, and the threat of capture had to be looming in all of their minds. Daniel wondered if they were criminals by trade or if this was a one-time deal.

The phone broke the silence once again with a steady ring.

Bethany held back and didn't move. She simply looked at the big man, apparently waiting for permission before answering the phone or doing anything else. Daniel didn't blame her. The robber was an incredibly large man with heavily developed muscles and a threatening presence. He would be a dangerous foe in any situation, and in his current stance of agitation, it wasn't worth challenging him without a very good reason.

The phone stopped ringing, then started again after about thirty seconds or so. No one else said a word. The air felt heavy. Even the other hostages were smart enough to stay quiet and subdued.

Finally, the bodybuilder relented. He motioned with his weapon toward the phone, then started pacing in front of the hostages, glaring at them as he did so. "Fine, answer the stupid phone and do whatever you want to do with J.P., but I'm not taking the blame. When the boss finds out, it'll be you who answers to him. Not me."

Bethany nodded and swung her rifle behind her,

then walked over and quickly picked up the receiver. "Yeah?"

She was silent as she listened, then turned and looked into the other robber's eyes as she spoke. "Look, we've got a man down. He's been shot, and he needs a doctor. I want you to send in someone to get him. One man and a stretcher. That's it."

She listened again and then stood straighter as her eyes narrowed. "No, I'm not letting a hostage take him outside. You're going to send in one EMT with a stretcher on wheels and he's going to come in and get the guy, and then he's going to turn around and leave. If he's armed, I'll kill him. If he does anything foolish, I'll kill him. Got it?"

She listened some more and then slammed down the phone and turned to the bodybuilder. "Okay, they're sending in a guy with a stretcher. Can you let him in the front door?"

The big robber blew out a breath, then nodded. "Yeah, I guess. The boss is going to blow a gasket over this. Cover me while I work."

J.P. groaned loudly. "Don't hand me over to them." He tried to sit up again but failed miserably. "I'll get you back, Hailey. I promise you that."

Daniel was surprised that the wounded man said Bethany's undercover name out loud. Hailey must be what Bethany was calling herself these days. He could tell it was a major breach of etiquette for the robbers to mention names because even the bodybuilder balked at his words.

"Shut up, man. Just close your mouth and keep it closed."

Daniel watched as the bodybuilder slung his rifle behind him and went to the front door and undid some wires, apparently disarming the bomb temporarily so the doors could be opened. Then he released the cables that were holding the door shut and opened one of them. A man dressed as an emergency tech pushed in a yellow stretcher on wheels, noticed the man lying on the floor and rushed to his side, but Bethany frisked him before she let him get close to the wounded man, and she searched the bags he brought in, presumably for any weapons or other suspicious devices. Meanwhile, the bodybuilder robber stayed near the front door and pulled his gun back around to the front and held it ready, his eyes following the EMT's every movement.

When the EMT approached him, J.P. started thrashing his arms around, trying to keep the EMT away from him. Bethany pointed her weapon at Daniel and motioned toward the fallen man. "Hey, hero. Help him get that man on the stretcher. Now."

Daniel nodded and moved quickly to help the EMT, glad that Bethany had allowed him to help. He glanced at the rest of the hostages as he did so, but although a few were watching the scene unfold, most were turned away and trying to stay as uninvolved as possible. It was probably wise of them not to challenge the robbers like he had, but doing nothing went against his basic ideals, and he knew Bethany was a cop, which gave him the advantage. He was also driven to help resolve this problem and was grateful to play even a small part in the resolution. He grabbed and secured the injured man's hands and helped lift him to the stretcher, being careful of the man's wound as he did so. Then he continued holding the man steady as the EMT strapped him to the gurney. Once the injured man couldn't pull away or fight any longer, the EMT checked his wound and re-bandaged it, then started an IV.

"Is he going to live?" Bethany asked.

"Looks like it," the EMT answered. "You called us just in time. He's lost a lot of blood and is in shock, but the hospital is close. I think he'll make it."

Bethany nodded, but kept her gun trained on the tech even as he spoke to her. She even kept it on him as he turned and pushed the gurney back out through the front door. Once he was gone, the bodybuilder lost no time in rewiring the door and securing the door handles with the cables.

"Why don't you let the women go?" Daniel asked quietly. "You'll still have plenty of hostages…"

Bethany swung around and pointed her weapon right at Daniel's chest. "Shut up." She motioned toward the line of hostages. "Sit back down and keep quiet."

He put up his hands again but didn't obey. "Look, you just did something decent. Don't stop now. Let the women go. You'll still have all of the men…"

The bodybuilder advanced quicker than Daniel had expected and loomed above him, his weapon once again pulled back like a club. "She told you to sit down and shut up. I've had enough of you and your mouth.

Do you hear me? Do as she says, buddy, or I'll make you comply. Got it?"

Daniel backed down and sat on the floor again, but he kept his eyes on Bethany. She had done the right thing by getting the injured man to safety, but how far was she going to take this robbery? She could put an end to it right now if she wanted to, and with his help, they could arrest the bodybuilder and catch the robbers in the vault unprepared and unaware. What was holding her back? Was she actually going to see this robbery through to the end? A chill went through him as he considered the possibilities. What was their endgame? What was the bigger picture that the body-builder had alluded to earlier? He didn't want to blow her cover, but he didn't want anyone else to get hurt either. As long as the robbers were in the bank, more violence could erupt at any moment.

Bethany's teeth chattered and she realized they had turned off the heat in the building and the temperature was slowly dropping. She'd given up her hoodie to make bandages for J.P., and the T-shirt she was wearing did little to stave off the cold. They were going straight down the law enforcement playbook. Step one was make them uncomfortable by cutting off the heat. Step two was keep the communication lines open while SWAT got into place in case a tactical operation was required. She was sure they already had snipers in place, looking for a clear shot if the negotiator couldn't talk them out of the building.

She glanced around the bank's interior and noticed

all of the Christmas decorations for the first time. Wreaths were placed under each teller station, and candles with pine cones and ribbon decorated some of the counters. She had been so wrapped up in this robbery that she hadn't given much thought to the season. Christmas had always been her favorite holiday—that is, until she and Daniel had broken up last year just a few days before the special day had arrived. She stole a look in his direction. He was still as attractive as ever, with dark hair in a short military cut and piercing blue eyes. His features were clearly defined, and he had a strong jaw and firm chin. He took good care of himself, and his athletic build showed it. She wondered if he still ran five miles every morning the way he had back when they were together. He had been on a serious health kick back then and played basketball with his squad on a regular basis. If she had to guess, she'd bet he had probably thrown himself into his exercise routines with gusto after their breakup. That had always been his way of dealing with stress or problems in his life as long as she'd known him.

She turned, trying to push the memories away. Their relationship was over and had been for over a year. She didn't need to be wallowing in the past; she needed to be looking forward. She wished he wasn't here now, forcing these memories to come flooding back in the middle of this operation. Once this undercover assignment was over, she would have her pick of assignments. Maybe it would be better if she moved out of state and started over someplace where there was no possibility of ever running into him again. Yes, that was a good plan. She'd heard Florida was nice this time of year. Or maybe South Carolina near the beach…

The phone rang again, bringing her out of her reverie. Terrell nodded at her, tacitly giving her permission to answer it. She slung her rifle to her back and walked over to the phone, then picked up the receiver.

"Hello," she answered.

"Your man is doing well," Sergeant Michaels stated.

"Good to know," Bethany answered.

"Can your boss come to the phone now?"

Bethany looked toward the back of the bank, but there had been no news from the vault. She assumed the rest of the robbers were still working on opening it. "Nope."

"Well, I need to get the rest of those hostages out of there before someone else gets hurt. What can I do to help move this along?"

"Sit tight and wait," she replied caustically. "We'll be out of your hair soon enough."

Sergeant Michaels seemed undaunted. "You have eighteen hostages. What would it take to get you to release ten of them?" Bethany's gut tightened. She wanted the people out of danger, but she worried about moving forward with the negotiations without Jackson's approval. He was already going to be upset that J.P. was gone. He might get even angrier if she went in the back to talk to him and interrupted his work while he was trying to open the vault. Jackson was usually a benevolent leader, but he was sometimes hard to read, and she never knew what was going to set him off. When he did get angry, his actions were often unexpected and violent. This robbery had already gone down a road they hadn't expected. She suddenly found herself in an uncomfortable position but didn't know quite how to get out of it.

Lost in thought, Bethany didn't answer, so Sergeant Michaels pushed forward. "Look, Bonnie. You probably realize we have an entry team ready to roll. We also have snipers in place, but we don't want to use force. We want this to end peacefully. Tell me what I need to do to make that happen."

Bethany was stuck. She knew that if she didn't give Sergeant Michaels something, it was going to push law enforcement into acting sooner than they wanted them to, and Jackson apparently needed more time to work on the vault. Michaels was also right about one thing. If the robbers and the police did have a confrontation, more violence was going to erupt. "Alright. We got in here before we ate lunch, and now you've got us freezing because you turned off the heat. Turn the heat back on and send in some pizzas, and I'll give you five hostages. That's the deal, and it's not negotiable." She hung up, trying to stay in character. Terrell was watching her every move, and the last thing she wanted was to make him suspicious. Too late, she realized Terrell's eyes had narrowed and his back had stiffened. He was angry once again.

"You're giving away hostages? Who put you in charge?" He stood and walked toward her, his stance threatening. Had she blown her cover, or was he just angry about her involving the hostages? A sliver of fear went down her spine as she replayed the words she'd spoken in her mind. Little details mattered in undercover work. One slip and it could mean her life. She knew that a single misstep or, even in some circles, mispronunciation could set off alarm bells, and she couldn't afford to have even little finger cymbals going off. She needed to be constantly without any suspicion whatsoever.

"First you give them J.P., and now you're giving them five more? Why? What's wrong with you?"

"Hey," she answered defensively, staying in character. "You're the one who told me to answer the phone. I'm just following your instructions and keeping the cops busy while we get into that vault, and I don't want to go back to the vault and interrupt them in the middle of their work either. If you want to talk to the guy on the phone instead of me, be my guest. They're threatening to bust in here with an assault team, not to mention taking potshots at us with snipers. Feel free to start negotiating with them instead of me any time you want. I'm just trying to buy the boss enough time to get the job done."

Terrell stopped a few steps away from her, his weapon held tightly in his hands. "No one put you in charge," he said, his tone deceptively soft and threatening. "You shouldn't be giving those cops anything. Jackson said our job was just to keep the hostages quiet. That's it. Now, because of you, J.P. has been arrested and you've got someone coming in here delivering pizza. Did you order extra cheese?" Now his voice was dripping with sarcasm.

"The boss didn't know the police were going to

threaten to burst in, or that J.P. was going to get shot. Now he's alive because of me. Don't forget that," she said, straightening and meeting his eye.

"Yeah, well, I would have just let him die. For all we know, he's out there singing like a bird, giving them a complete list of our members including birth dates and shoe sizes. You've put this job in jeopardy." He took a step closer. "You put the organization in jeopardy."

FIVE

Bethany's heart started beating faster as Terrell's anger consumed him. The pressure had to be getting to him, and the way he was griping the rifle was starting to make her nervous. It wasn't unheard of for robbers to turn on each other during the middle of a job, and for the second time in only a matter of minutes, she felt like she was in real danger. Terrell had always seemed levelheaded to her in the past, but stress and fear could change that like the flip of a switch. She was walking a thin line on this assignment by participating in a crime of this magnitude. The stakes were already high, and they were getting higher by the minute.

"Hey, which five are you going to release?" Daniel asked, drawing Terrell's attention as he stood up and took a few steps toward Terrell. "You should let the women go—"

"You should shut up," Terrell said roughly as he once again turned his anger on Daniel. "I'm getting really tired of telling you to keep your mouth shut."

Bethany glanced at Daniel's eyes and understood that he was giving her the perfect opportunity to look tough and convince Terrell that her persona was real. She was instantly both grateful to him and angry with him. She could take care of herself. She didn't want him to put himself in danger for her sake. Before Terrell could act, she stepped in between them and pushed Daniel back. "Hey, hero, haven't we told you about a hundred times to sit down and shut up?" She pulled her rifle back and hit him in the gut, then as he bent over, she hit him over the back. Her blows looked good but actually had very little force behind them, so she did little to no damage. Thankfully, Daniel seemed to instantly understand what she was doing and did a good job of acting and responding to her actions. He ended up on the floor, clutching his stomach and rolling as if the force of her blows had severely injured him. When he landed, he hit his nose awkwardly, which caused it to start bleeding. The sight of the blood made the entire scene seem more real, and Terrell bought it all, hook, line and sinker. He reached for Bethany as if to stop her, but she pulled her foot back and gave Daniel several vicious kicks in the abdomen before Terrell actually succeeded in grabbing her shoulders and pulling her back from the victim on the ground.

"Are you trying to kill him? Good grief, girl. We agreed we weren't going to kill anyone. Didn't you just give me a speech about how important it was to save someone's life? Leave that guy alone!"

Bethany didn't want to point out to Terrell that two short minutes ago he had been threatening both her and Daniel with violence. Daniel moaned loudly, and Bethany put her foot on his pelvis and pushed him over on his chest to lessen the noise.

"You said I was putting the operation in jeopardy," she spat. "But I'm just as committed to the cause as you are, and if I need to kill this guy to prove it to you, then that's what I'm going to do." She tried to pull away from Terrell, but he held her fast and turned her to face him so their eyes met.

"Back off. I was out of line. Look, why don't you take this guy back to the bathroom and clean him up. We don't want to leave anyone in that condition when we clear out of here."

"You clean him up," she said severely as she slung her rifle on to her back. "What do I care what he looks like?"

Terrell released her and straightened. Apparently, he wasn't willing to go that far, or he didn't like her saucy mouth. Either way, he wanted his command obeyed. "I told you to do it, and I meant it. I'll stay out here and keep an eye on things. You don't know how to operate the charges on the front door. I do. If something happens, I need to be here."

"What about them?" She swung her rifle toward the hostages and a few of them whimpered at her implied threat.

"I'll shoot any of them who move a muscle."

"Fine." She shrugged as if the time with Daniel didn't matter, but she was secretly pleased. She had been trying to figure out a way to talk to him in private anyway, to explain to him what was going on, and this situation had worked out perfectly. She nudged Daniel with her shoe and he moaned in response. "Let's go, hero."

He cringed as if he was afraid of her touch, and

Bethany silently thanked him for putting on such a realistic performance. She nudged him again. "I said, let's go, hero." She handed Terrell her rifle and then reached down to help Daniel up. He looked at her suspiciously when she offered her arm but eventually reached out and grabbed her right wrist, and she pulled him to his feet. As soon as he was vertical, she put his arm around her shoulders and wedged herself under his arm so she could support him as he walked. They made slow progress without saying a word until they had entered the family bathroom and flipped on the light. Bethany pulled the door closed and let him ease against the sink. Then she pulled her mask up and left it sitting above her head. It felt good to finally get out of the sweaty thing. She leaned against the door frame and watched as Daniel turned on the water and started rinsing the blood from his face.

"I'm sorry if I hurt you, Daniel."

He continued washing his face but eventually grabbed the paper towel she offered and dried his face. "When?"

She raised her eyebrows. "What do you mean *when*?"

"You're sorry you hurt me just now, or when you disappeared without a trace a year ago?" He tossed the paper towel away, straightened and gave her a small smile.

Bethany narrowed her eyes. Good grief! He wanted to have this conversation now? "Hey now. The way I remember it, we both decided it was over last year. It was a mutual decision."

"No," he said softly, "we had an argument. We both said things we regretted, and you didn't give us an opportunity to fix it. Instead, you disappeared." He paused. "I've missed you, you know."

Bethany tapped the lid down on her emotions. There was an element of truth to what he said, but she didn't want to examine it. She didn't even want to have this discussion—not now, and not ever. The scars had already healed over. She didn't want to reopen the wounds. "Maybe I didn't want to fix it," she said back, her tone derisive. "We were over, Daniel. You just didn't want to accept it."

He looked up quickly. "That's not how I remember it."

His eyes met hers and contained a pain that she hadn't expected. She looked away first, unable to bear the look in his eyes. "I am sorry, Daniel, both for today and for a year ago. I didn't want to hurt you. I never meant to do that."

He gently grasped her arm, then touched her chin and turned her head to look at him again. His touch sent a shiver down her spine. "I looked for you for months. I watched your apartment. I searched high and low. Why do you say we were over? We were just beginning."

He leaned forward as if to kiss her, but she pulled her head away. She did not want to continue this conversation. He was forcing her to feel things she didn't want to feel. It was safer all around if they left the past in the past. "We can't talk about this now. Terrell is waiting for us."

* * *

A wave of frustration swept through Daniel, and he realized he wasn't going to get the answers he was seeking. At least not today. Bethany's heart may have closed over, but he had never stopped loving her. How could he help her see that? He had seen fear in her eyes that long ago day, and the fear was back today. What was she afraid of? Had they gotten too serious, too soon? Is that why she had run away? He remembered the day she had driven off and disappeared from his life, the angry words still on both of their tongues. He should have gone after her, but he'd always thought they'd have another opportunity to talk and sort things out, and he thought waiting for them both to cool down was the wiser course. Apparently, he had been very, very wrong. But even so, it wasn't in him to give up. He might not be able to convince her to return to him, but before he let her go, he at least wanted to understand what had happened and why. He leaned back against the sink. "Then when can we talk? You're obviously undercover. When does this assignment end? Will you disappear again once they've brought you home?"

He saw the answer in her eyes. She would leave as soon as it was over, and she wasn't going to contact him. Exasperation and the fear of losing her once again caused a tightening in his chest. "Bethany, please. At least give me an opportunity to talk to you before you take another assignment."

"I don't know when this will end…"

"But it will, at some point. Please promise me we'll talk."

She said nothing in response, and it was obvious she wasn't going to say another word on the subject. His face was throbbing and he touched his nose gingerly. "I think I broke my nose."

A look of worry crossed her face, and she tore off another paper towel, wet it and handed it to him. "I'm sorry. Here. You're still bleeding."

He took the paper towel from her and put his head back, hoping to staunch the flow. "Can I have my gun back?"

"Sorry, no, at least not yet. Someone might have seen me take it, and I don't want to blow my cover. You have my word though that I'll get it back to you as soon as I can."

"So your handler approved a bank robbery?"

"Yeah, there's a bigger picture here that we've been investigating for about a year."

He brought his head back down. "Care to share?"

She gave him a small laugh. "You know the rules. I can't do that."

"How can you stand to be a part of this? I've never done undercover work—I'll admit it. And I respect those of you that do. I just don't think I could get past the crimes going on all around me. I mean, a man got shot out there. That's got to be tough."

She leaned back against the door frame, giving him an expression that showed she was pleased with his interest. Her work had always been very important to her. Sometimes he thought she liked being an FBI agent more than any other aspect of her life. "I look for the gray and stay away from the black and white.

There's usually something good about a person, even if they are a criminal, so I focus on that aspect of their personality. Criminals can tell if I'm scared, and they know if I'm being judgmental about their lifestyle. I have to show them that I see them as a person, not just as someone doing bad things. Take Terrell." She nodded toward the door.

"You mean that big bodybuilder guy?"

"Yeah, that's the one. He loves dogs. Can you believe it? He saw a stray the other day that almost got hit by a car, and he made us stop, right there in the middle of the road, so he could grab the dog off the street. Then we had to change all of our plans, turn around and head in the opposite direction, just so he could drop the dog off at his sister's so she could find a good home for it. How crazy is that?"

Daniel smiled. He was glad she was talking to him, even if she wasn't willing to discuss their relationship. Something was better than nothing. "I can't imagine that big guy caring that much."

"Neither could I, but since I love dogs myself, it makes it much easier to be around him now that I've seen that side of his personality. We've found some common ground." She sighed. "This is a really important assignment. I've been thrown into the deep end of one of the region's most dangerous criminal organizations, and I really want a win so I can put an end to their activities. By the time I'm through with this, I hope to bring down some of the most powerful people in the state. This investigation reaches all the way up to the senator's office."

Daniel could hear the passion in her voice, yet the fact that they were committing a crime here today still didn't sit right with him. "I understand, but is it ethically okay to rob a bank to reach that objective? I know you're in deep, but isn't this going too far?"

"This isn't just an adrenaline-filled journey I'm on, Daniel. I'll be able to trace the money we steal today and get the final pieces to the puzzle. They've been building a war chest for a reason, and we need to know why. They're planning something big, something that's going to do a lot more damage than a bank robbery and will hurt a lot more people in the long run. I know it's dangerous, but my handler and I both thought it was worth the risk."

Daniel could see that he would never win this argument. And he had to admit, undercover cops were some of the bravest people he had ever worked with. Bethany wasn't short on guts or determination. She was a dedicated, hardworking FBI agent who got the job done. "Well I just don't want to see you go native and get caught up in this lifestyle. I would hate to visit you behind bars."

She smiled, a smile that always made his gut tighten. She was so beautiful, and her beauty was so much more than skin-deep. "No worries. I'm still a cop when I go to bed at night. I'm not switching sides." She motioned toward the door. "We'd better get back out there before Terrell comes in here looking for us." She pulled the mask back down to cover her face.

"Do you guys have an exit strategy?"

"You bet. And no one will get hurt. I promise."

He let her wedge herself under his arm again, and he took a wounded stance so they could return to the bank lobby. He was fine with acting the injured party as long as it helped keep her safe. He just hoped she could keep her promise.

SIX

Jackson was pacing in front of the group of hostages when Bethany and Daniel returned to the lobby. She noticed that he and the other robbers had several bags at their feet—hopefully full of cash that they had taken from the vault. She led Daniel over to the line of hostages, dropped him unceremoniously on the floor, then retrieved her weapon from Terrell and joined the group of robbers. She tried to act nonchalant and not attract attention to herself as she took her place with the other robbers.

"Where have you been?" Jackson asked when he got her attention. He had a suspicious look on his face, and she hurried to reassure him.

"Cleaning up a mess," she responded tightly, but in a voice that was still low enough for only the group of robbers to hear.

There was still an apprehensive look in Jackson's eyes. "Where is J.P.? Did I understand correctly that you let the cops in here while I was in the back working on the vault?"

A sliver of fear washed over her when she saw Jackson's eyes narrow and darken as he spoke. He was pacing nervously, and his hands were fisting and releasing over and over again. Had she blown it? The last thing she needed was for Jackson to get suspicious of her and find out she was really an FBI agent at this late date in the game. Still, she stiffened her spine and pushed forward. He had always respected strength during their relationship. That's what she would show him now at this critical juncture. "He was going to die without help," she said roughly, her tone matter-of-fact. "His wound was serious, and he'd lost too much blood. He was going into shock."

"And being a doctor, you'd know what shock looks like, right?" His voice was derisive.

She deliberately softened her speech but still spoke with authority. "I may not be a doctor, but I'm also not an idiot. Shock isn't too hard to identify, and neither is a large pool of blood on the floor. I happen to value life. J.P. is a true believer. He's a valuable asset to the cause. I wanted to save him."

Jackson took a threatening step toward her, but she still didn't back down. "That was my call, not yours. I wasn't in China. All you had to do was come back and ask."

His words made her heart beat even faster. It had taken months to gain Jackson's trust. She'd had an informant introduce them, and from there, she'd become a provider for Jackson, bringing him electronics and other "stolen" items that she claimed she'd gotten from other jobs she'd pulled around town. They were actually items provided by the FBI, but they had been good enough to please Jackson. She had quickly gained the reputation as someone who could lay her hands on whatever the group needed. She had even given him the latest and greatest cell phone, which, unknown to Jackson, included a bugging device that allowed the FBI to track Jackson and listen in on his conversations. Despite this track record of success, her elevated status could disappear in an instant if Jackson began to suspect her. She decided a strategic retreat was in order.

"You're right, Jackson. I should have asked. I'm sorry. I don't want to do anything that would jeopardize the mission."

"Did you consider that now the cops might be able to get him to talk? He could blow our entire operation."

She shook her head. "I was just trying to save his life. I didn't think. I really am sorry." Her heart continued its pounding for another very long moment as she watched Jackson consider her words. Even the rest of the team were all silent and completely still as they watched and waited for a cue from Jackson. Terrell's face had a look that said *I told you so* written all over it, but to his credit, he said nothing.

Finally, Jackson shrugged, and the rest of the group followed his lead and relaxed, as well. She let out a breath in relief as he spoke. "Next time, ask me. I'm in charge. Got it? There's a lot riding on this. Our friends are counting on us."

"Yes, I get it. Definitely." She tried to change the subject and hoped he wouldn't notice. "Were you successful with the vault?"

"Of course," he answered with a sly smile. "Did you doubt me?"

She shook her head. "Not even for a minute."

"Did the cops call back since they took J.P.?"

"Yeah," Bethany answered. "They think we're trading five hostages for pizzas and having them turn the heat back on. I had to give them something to work on. They were getting antsy and threatening to send in a strike team if I didn't agree to something."

Jackson raised an eyebrow but didn't comment, which made Bethany nervous again. Finally, he shrugged once, then took a step back and addressed the group, apparently putting her negotiations with the police behind them. She was glad to see that he was ready to move on. The last few minutes had been extremely uncomfortable for her, and she was ready to get out of this bank. "Let's go, folks. We're ready for phase three."

Bethany knew that phase three meant they were putting their escape plan into action. She glanced over at Daniel, glad that this robbery was finally coming to an end. Soon they would be gone, and the pain this encounter had caused him to relive would end. She hoped he could move on and find some measure of peace once she disappeared again. There was no reason for them to see each other once her team of robbers escaped, and she wished him well on whatever path he chose to follow.

She turned back to Jackson, who was talking to Terrell. "Get those hostages in the back room and lock the door. The rest of you, come with me."

Terrell nodded, turned to the hostages and started barking out orders. "Okay, everyone stand up!"

He started pacing in front of the group, waving his weapon up and down to encourage them to move faster. The faces of the hostages showed their trepidation, but they quickly obeyed and stood up against the wall.

Daniel stood with the rest of them, glad that this episode would soon be over but still fighting the host of sensations that seeing Bethany had evoked. Once the robbers escaped, would he see her again? Bethany hadn't committed to any future conversations with him, and he had no idea when her current assignment would end. When it did, for all he knew, she would accept a post in a city on the other side of the United States. How had things gone so badly between them? One moment, they were in love and planning their wedding and the next, she was gone. A sense of emptiness swept over him and he sighed inwardly, knowing there wasn't anything he could do to change the status quo. At this point, it looked like he would probably never even get an opportunity to try.

Suddenly a shot rang out and one of the female hostages pointed at Terrell and screamed. Daniel's eyes followed the woman's pointing finger and saw Terrell's body crumple to the floor. Within seconds, more shots rang out, and Jackson's body also hit the floor, as well as the robber's with the limp. Daniel didn't think. He was only a few feet away from Bethany, and he took a running dive toward her and hit her hard, taking her to the ground. She wasn't wearing the black hoodie like the other robbers and in a perfect world, the snipers all knew that she was law enforcement. But on the off chance that no one knew the truth, he wanted her out of the line of fire just in case.

He heard a bullet whiz by only inches from where their heads had just been. They hit the floor hard and once they landed, they slid for several inches on the slick tile before coming to a stop near a small table. Bethany lost her grip on her rifle when they hit the floor and it landed a few feet away, out of reach. Daniel felt the air whoosh out of both of their bodies due to the force of the fall. Total chaos ensued all around them.

Oh, dear God. Please don't let Bethany be dead. His prayer was short but intense. He moved closer and tried to feel her pulse. "Are you okay?" He crouched above her protectively, trying to shield her from any other flying bullets or danger.

Bethany didn't answer, and he wasn't even sure she'd heard him. Women were screaming, and several policemen had come in the bank through the ceiling, rappelling in full battle gear and wielding weapons just seconds after the first shot had been fired.

"Bethany?" Daniel couldn't find a pulse, but his hands were shaking. He shook her gently but still got no response. In fact, she wasn't even moving. Fear gripped his heart. Had he been too late? He shifted, trying to get in a position where he could remove her mask and check her vitals and repeated his prayer.

"Freeze!" A SWAT officer was suddenly standing over them, his weapon pointed at Bethany only inches from her head. He had steel gray eyes and a two-inch scar on his chin. A few seconds later, another officer joined him, this one pointing his weapon at Daniel.

"I'm a detective," Daniel responded. "My name is Daniel Morley. My shield is in my left front pocket. Can I get it out and show you?"

The more recently arrived SWAT officer motioned with his rifle. "Slowly."

Daniel carefully moved to Bethany's side and gradually pulled his shield out of his pocket and offered it up for inspection. The officer Daniel had now nicknamed Scar took it and looked at it cautiously while the other kept his weapon trained on Bethany, who was still lying motionless on the floor. Satisfied, he handed it back.

"Okay, Detective. Move away from the suspect."

Daniel slowly did so, but he was getting more and more worried about Bethany by the second. She still hadn't moved since he'd tackled her. Had she been hit by the sniper? Had her head hit the ground when they'd landed? Why wasn't she moving? There was a lot of noise and general confusion in the bank, but he tuned it all out and was entirely focused on her.

Was she even breathing? He couldn't tell. His heart seemed to stop beating. Had she been killed like the others? He didn't see any blood, but he couldn't see all of her, and her mask still covered her face. Had he been too late?

Scar leaned over and pulled off Bethany's mask while the other SWAT officer kept his rifle trained on her prone body. It came off easily, and Daniel breathed a sigh of relief when it didn't reveal any injury on her face or head.

She must have been unconscious, but then abruptly she moaned and moved slightly, causing both officers to stiffen and move closer with their weapons. "Freeze!" they both ordered in unison.

She opened her eyes and took a moment to focus as she slowly recuperated and returned to the here and now.

"Hands out to your sides," Scar ordered. She slowly complied, and once her arms were parallel to her body, they kicked her feet apart until she was spread eagle on the ground. She glanced at Daniel but said nothing.

Daniel wanted to protest their rough treatment of her, but he still couldn't blow her cover. That was for her to do at the correct moment when she felt like she was out of danger, or for her handler to do once she was arrested. Whatever the case, there were protocols to be followed, and now was not the time or place to notify them of her FBI status.

While Scar pointed his rifle at her, the other officer frisked her for other weapons, then roughly flipped her over on her stomach. They found his service revolver that was still in the waistband of her pants and pulled another small revolver out of her right boot. They also pulled a small knife out of her left boot.

"Got any other hardware we should know about?"

She still said nothing, but shook her head. As Daniel watched, the officer pulled her hands roughly behind her back, handcuffed her and yanked her to her feet.

"You have the right to remain silent…"

As soon as they finished going through her Miranda rights, the two men led her out of the bank.

Daniel watched her go, surprised at how much things had changed in the last fifteen minutes. He felt like he was on a wild roller coaster ride that was both terrifying and exhilarating at the same time.

He had lost her again. But a lot of his questions had been answered. And for the next few hours, he knew where he could find her.

And there was a possibility, ever so small, that he might be able to see her again.

SEVEN

"I can't believe you killed them all. Good grief! One entire year of investigation ruined!" Bethany's handler, Justin Harper, banged his hand on the conference room table, and three of the individuals in the room jumped in response to the noise. "What is wrong with you people!" He had a handful of folders in his arms, and he called off the names as he slammed each folder down on the table in front of him.

"Terrell Mason, shot dead. Jackson Smith, shot dead. John Hoss, shot dead. And let's not forget, if not for the quick thinking of Detective Morley here, you would have also shot my special agent through the head, as well!"

"Hold on now," Captain Dennis Murphy intoned, leaning back in his chair. "The communication failures weren't all on our end. We didn't even hear about this operation until we were on our way in. You should have let us know you had an operation in the works months ago, and that you had an agent in the field committing armed robbery. How did you expect us to react?

Roll out a red carpet for the robbers and let them reel the money out in golden wheelbarrows? We followed standard operating procedure. SOP. Sir." He banged the table himself as he said each letter. "Do not lay your gross failures at our feet."

Bethany flicked her nails, incredibly tired of the blame game going on in front of her. They had already been sitting here for over an hour, and they still hadn't gotten anywhere. She was just as angry as her handler, but she was not convinced that a show of rage and frustration was going to further this meeting. The bottom line was that people in both agencies had screwed up, and the mistakes had almost been at the cost of her life. It had also cost her all the progress she'd made in the investigation, and she wasn't sure it was salvageable. She had spent an entire year infiltrating that group, and for what? The leader, Jackson Smith, was dead, and he was the one who had trusted her and had been the source of information that she had been using to build her case against the entire criminal organization.

She glanced around the room at the various faces. It had been quite a few months since she had seen the inside of a police station, not to mention a conference room. Many of these people she'd never seen before. Both the local and federal law enforcement agencies had a contingency at the table, and both the state district attorney's office and the federal attorney general's office had sent a team, as well. Captain Murphy had brought Daniel and his assistant, a petite African-American lady who was furiously scribbling notes on a legal pad and trying to look unobtrusive. So far, she hadn't said a single word and if Bethany had to guess, she doubted the woman would speak a single syllable during the entire meeting. Sergeant Michaels, the hostage negotiator she had talked to on the phone during the robbery, was present as well, but he had also said very little. Apparently, he was content to have his captain do the talking. He seemed more like a man of action rather than a verbose member of the team, and he kept watching the clock as if he had someplace else to be.

Her eyes roamed over to Justin Harper, her handler. She hadn't known him very well before they were assigned to work together on this detail, but he had been reliable to date and good about providing the products and intelligence she needed to worm her way into Jackson's cell within the criminal organization. She glanced over at his assistant, a young man with shortly cropped blond hair and stunning green eyes named Max Westfield. Westfield was the newest member of the team and had only been there for a couple of months. He was also taking notes, but he was typing on a tablet computer, and occasionally looking around the room at the various occupants as if he were taking the measure of each of them. Despite the intriguing color of his eyes, Bethany was a bit repelled by the man. It wasn't so much anything Westfield had said or done; in fact, he had been very courteous. He just seemed to be watching her constantly and was almost flirtatious in his looks and actions. She may be single, but she certainly wasn't looking for a relationship. She wondered if he would get the message through her body language, or if she would actually have to say something to him to make him move on to somebody else. She hoped it was the former. She didn't relish a confrontation with him.

"How did you even plan on getting out of that bank alive?" Captain Murphy asked, finally addressing Bethany for the first time during the meeting. She looked up, surprised, and put an end to her woolgathering. "Explosives, sir. I'm sure you found the C-4 in some of the duffel bags that were still in the bank. That building was built over a crawl space, which easily accessed the laundry room of the apartment building to the north, which led to the parking garage directly northwest of that location. We had a van ready and waiting to go on the bottom level of the parking deck. I'm sure it's been moved by now by others from the group, but we figured it would take us approximately twelve minutes to get from the bank to the van through access tunnels that we'd completed over the last few weeks. It was going to be a bit tricky to ferry the money over there because of the weight, but the operation was certainly doable for a group of motivated bank robbers."

"What about the hostages?"

"What about them?" she asked, raising an eyebrow.

"What were your plans for them?" he asked, leaning forward. His stance was aggressive, but instead of taking offense at his behavior, she decided to lean back and speak softer, hoping not to engage the man and make matters even worse. She had already listened to the yelling for an hour. Her ears hurt. All of the bravado and posturing was giving her a headache. With each new argument, she was beginning to appreciate her undercover assignment more and more. It had been good to be away from the politics and office maneuvering that was apparently required in order to succeed.

"We never wanted anyone to get injured, sir. That was the plan from the beginning and, of course, the FBI would never have signed off on the robbery if the hostages had been at risk. Once the vault was breeched, our plan was to lock the hostages in the back of the bank in the conference room and leave them there during the explosion and the escape. They wouldn't have been impacted by the detonation."

Captain Murphy stood quickly, put up his hands and took a couple of steps in her direction. "Now hold on just a minute. You don't call firing high-powered weapons near innocent people putting them at risk?" he yelled.

"No, sir," she responded calmly. "I was constantly with the hostages, and I had a high-powered weapon myself so I could stop any trouble before it started. I kept them where I could see them at all times for exactly that reason."

Captain Murphy pointed toward Daniel. "What about my detective's nose?"

She'd had enough. What did the man expect? A perfect operation? A golden guarantee? If he wanted to find fault, he needed to point that finger back at himself and his own operation. After all, she was the one who had almost been killed. "What about it, Captain? I am sorry about Detective Morley's nose, I truly am, but he's alive, isn't he? That's more than I could have said if he hadn't been there when your team came storming into that bank. They would have killed me if he hadn't knocked me to the ground in the nick of time. Detective Morley saved my life. That's something I won't soon forget, but it sure would be nice if you remembered that it was your men who killed the rest of the suspects and tried to take me out, as well."

Captain Murphy's face turned red. "I've never heard such insolence! You just hold it right there, Special Agent—"

Daniel stood and held up his hands. "Captain, please. I know I'm outranked by most of the people at this table, and until now I've been quietly sitting here listening to everyone's point of view, but I was there, in the bank, and I can tell you what happened from my firsthand experience. Since we've finally gotten around to my injury and my role in the operation, I think I've earned a chance to speak." His voice was soft yet in control, and Bethany admired the way he showed a quiet strength. He didn't need the bluster that the captain showed to get his point across or the threats and anger that her handler kept throwing around. His tone was matter-of-fact and to the point. "We seem to keep talking about this in the past tense, but to my way of thinking, this operation isn't over, not by a long shot. I don't know all of the details or the background information, but I do know Special Agent Walker. I know her level of commitment and I know this is an important undercover operation that has high stakes. We may have lost a golden opportunity by killing Jackson Smith and his cohorts, and I don't know the ins and outs of the organization that Agent Walker is infiltrating, but

I do know that we aren't out of options, at least not yet. I suggest we move forward as a team. We can't forget that J.P., the robber that got shot, is still in the hospital. As far as he knows, three of the robbers were shot and killed. He doesn't know that Bethany survived, or why. We can use that fact to our advantage."

Bethany nodded, her excitement starting to grow as she began to understand the idea that Daniel seemed to be suggesting. "You're right. We can tell him that when the police stormed in, I was in the bathroom cleaning you up. I pulled off my mask and blended in with the other hostages…"

Captain Murphy snapped his fingers, apparently also grasping Daniel's train of thought. "And that's why you weren't arrested," he finished. "You were able to escape detection because you hid your mask and rifle and got lost in the general confusion that occurred when the bank got raided."

"But what about you?" Justin asked, motioning toward Daniel, his tone skeptical. "J.P. knows that you know she was a robber. He knows that you would have identified her to law enforcement when they came in. She couldn't have changed her clothes…"

"No," Daniel agreed, "but she could have let her hair down out of the ponytail, and without the mask she would have looked quite different. She also removed the hoodie when she was tending J.P.'s wounds. When people are stressed and in a difficult situation, they have trouble remembering details and might not have remembered what she was wearing underneath. The robbers were identified by their hoodies and masks."

"Are you willing to bet her life on that?" Justin said, his tone sharp. "I'm not. And I'm not sending her back into a dangerous situation without more. We need a stronger story. I know J.P. I helped compile the background on him. He's a hothead, but he's not an idiot. He'll see holes in any story that isn't a really good one, and that will put my agent in jeopardy. We can't give him some half-baked tale and hope he'll swallow it."

Daniel sat back down. Instead of looking discouraged, he seemed thoughtful. Didn't this guy ever give up? At least he was trying to help her make lemonade from a bowl of lemons. She had to appreciate his efforts. "I'm definitely not suggesting we put Special Agent Walker in danger either," he said. "If we need to come up with a better story, then we come up with a better story. We're an intelligent group of professionals here, ladies and gentlemen. I'm sure if we put our heads together, we can solve this problem. All I'm suggesting is that we move forward with the operation. We suffered a setback, yes, but we still can make this right."

"I have the solution."

All heads turned toward Captain Murphy, some with skeptical looks on their faces. His tone was more moderate, which Bethany appreciated, but when he spoke, his words shocked her. "The answer is simple. We send in Detective Morley undercover with her."

"What?" This time she stood. "Are you nuts?"

His head snapped toward her, and she instantly regretted her impetuous words. He was a captain after all, even if his idea was completely ludicrous.

"No, Agent, I'm not. Detective Morley is one of my

best. He can be brought up to speed on your case, and we can say he decided to join your group of robbers. Anti-government, aren't they?"

Daniel turned and looked at Bethany's expression. She was obviously not pleased that Captain Murphy had been so flippant with his comment about the group she had infiltrated. His captain was a good man, even if he was a little unpolished at times. He got the job done, and his superiors rewarded him for it, but he had never been known for his tact.

Bethany slowly retook her seat. "I meant no disrespect, sir. I agree that Detective Morley is outstanding at his job. My surprise was based upon your suggestion that he join my undercover operation. It took me over a year to gain their trust, and they are much more than an anti-government organization. It's a complicated belief system that goes back several generations and stretches into the members' livelihoods, even into how they raise their children. You don't just join the group. You live it."

"Believe it or not, agent, my people know a thing or two about police work. We may not have your FBI funding, but we do have the grit and determination it takes to do the job correctly."

"Sir…" she started to protest again and Daniel smiled inwardly. She wasn't going to be able to dig herself out of this hole, no matter how hard she tried. The captain had been offended, and there would be no soothing his pride, at least not today after all of the yelling and blame that had already been passed around.

"It makes a good legend, Agent," he said gruffly. He had enough rank that he could interrupt her with impunity. "He helped you escape because he believes in the cause. If both of you go in, you'll be less vulnerable because you can watch each other's backs."

Daniel shook his head. "That may not fly after what J.P. witnessed at the bank between us, sir, but we can figure something out. Give us some time to come up with some background scenarios, and we'll create a story that works." He glanced at Bethany. He could tell by her expression that she wasn't happy, but he was looking for any opportunity he could find to spend time with her, and if it took accepting an undercover operation to do it, then so be it. He had never wanted to do this type of job in the past, but he would do it now if it meant working with Bethany and getting a second chance to figure out what had gone wrong between them.

The group hashed out a few more details about the joint mission and then slowly started to break up and separate.

Max Westfield stopped Bethany as she was leaving the room and blocked her by the door. "I really admire you and the work you are doing. It's incredibly dangerous, but very worthwhile."

"Thank you, Mr. Westfield." She forced a smile at him but tried to push by. Daniel noticed this from across the conference room but was waylaid by the deputy attorney general, and although he could hear their conversation, he couldn't intervene.

She gave Max Westfield a tentative smile. "I appreciate your comments, Mr. Westfield, and your support. It is dangerous but if we are successful, it will all be worth it. Please excuse me." He moved a little closer and made it impossible for her to get by him. She actually took a step back and looked slightly uncomfortable.

"Please, call me Max. I might have some ideas for your backstory, if you want some help—"

She cut him off. "Thank you so much, but we have a team for that. I do appreciate the offer." She tried a second time to walk past him, but once again he blocked her path.

"I have a background in undercover work. I know I'm just an assistant right now, but I came from the New York field office where I did that kind of work, and I'm up for promotion."

She nodded. "I'm sure you did, but that's not the way we do things here. Like I said, I do appreciate the offer. Special Agent Harper is the boss, and we do things his way. You'll have to take this up with him."

Daniel finally excused himself from the attorney general and moved over to Westfield's side. "Agent Walker, I have a few things I'd like to discuss with you before you leave, if you have time," he said softly. "We need to get some details straight about this undercover operation."

"That would be fine. We can talk on my way out." She nodded at Westfield. "Thanks again." Westfield looked disappointed, but he finally stepped aside, glaring at Daniel as he did so.

"You know he was flirting with you," Daniel said

for her ears only once they were well away from the group.

"Of course," Bethany said, frowning a bit. "But he's not my type at all. He looks like he just graduated high school, and honestly, I think he's a bit too pushy." She smiled, but this time it was genuine. "Thankfully, I rarely have to deal with that guy."

Daniel didn't like that someone was flirting with her, but he did like the way that Bethany smiled. It lit up her entire face and brought out a small dimple on her cheek that was simply adorable. It was the first time he had seen her smile in quite some time. He wished she smiled more. "So what do you think about this undercover idea?"

Suddenly, the smile disappeared completely. She was obviously not pleased. "I think it's a mistake, just like I said during the meeting. It puts you in unnecessary danger, and me too if I have to babysit you."

Babysit? She felt like she had to babysit him? "Now hold on—"

"Look, don't let your male pride take a hit. That's not what I meant. You're a good cop. All I'm trying to say is that being undercover is hard enough when I have to watch out for myself. Everything I say and do is constantly being scrutinized. If you're there too, it's double the work and double the danger. You've also never done an assignment like this before. That makes it even more risky."

"Is the mission important?"

She frowned. "You know it is. I wouldn't have gone so far as participating in a bank robbery otherwise."

"Then let's do it. Together. Bring me up to speed, and let me do my job."

She paused as if considering his words, but it wasn't as if they had a choice. Their orders had already been decided. Still, he wanted her buy-in. "Look, I know I haven't done undercover before, but I'm not a rookie, Bethany. I won't let you down."

"I know you're good, Daniel. I've never doubted that. I'm just used to working alone."

He wanted to ask her if she had personal reasons for hesitating too, but now wasn't the time or place for that discussion. She hadn't wanted to talk about their past at the bank, and he knew intuitively that it was going to take time and effort to pry the answers out of her. One thing he did know though—she was worth the effort.

She met his eye. "Thanks for saving my life at the bank. I owe you one."

It was his turn to smile. "You're welcome. It was my pleasure."

She winked at him, then turned. "See you at the rendezvous location tomorrow at 9:00 a.m," she said with a wave.

He watched her leave, then left the building separately through a different side door.

Unfortunately, neither one of them noticed the people tailing them.

EIGHT

"You're going to have to pretend to be a dirty cop." Bethany sat back, running her hands through her hair and pulling it back from her face. "I just don't see another way around it." They were at a small diner in St. Elmo, a small neighborhood at the foot of Lookout Mountain, seated near the back where they had a good view of everyone in the restaurant, as well as everyone coming and going in the parking lot through the large picture window at the front. They had just spent the last two hours going over every detail, no matter how small, of the bank robbery and what the other hostages had witnessed during the various exchanges. They had also discussed what they thought J.P. had seen and heard, and how they could use him as the key to moving forward. He was the only real link left to the organization that Bethany still had, so she would have to use her relationship with J.P. to get back into the group. They were all hoping that bond was strong enough to allow her not only to get reconnected but also to bring Daniel into the fold.

"Being labeled as *dirty* really stinks, but I don't see any other option," Daniel agreed. "Too many of the other hostages know I was a cop or could find out by asking a few simple questions. They would all start to wonder how you escaped without me looking the other way."

Justin Harper, the third party at the table, nodded. "We just don't have time to put another cover story in place in time. You'll also have to use your own name. We can't come up with a believable legend for you after what happened at the bank." He took a drink of coffee. "Don't worry though. We'll be sure to restore your name and reputation once this mission is completed. For the time being, you've been temporarily assigned to the FBI task force. Captain Murphy knows, but no one else. Everyone else at the Chattanooga Police Department has been told that you've been assigned to a special detail and that's it. Keep the FBI connection to yourself."

"Bringing you on board might be easier than I originally thought," Bethany said as she took a sip of her hot chocolate. "We'll be offering them something—someone in law enforcement with an excellent reputation that they think they can manipulate. That's a big carrot. It also took them a year to trust me, but in their eyes, I'm Hailey Weber, a criminal with a spotty past. I had to prove myself. You, on, the other hand, already proved yourself by saving me at the bank."

"Do you think J.P. can get you the introductions you need?" Justin asked.

"That's the crux of the entire problem." She looked

to Daniel, who was hearing most of this information for the first time. "The organization is set up in cells. Jackson Smith was the head of our cell, but he was really the only one who had contact with the other cells. I was just getting to the point where I was trusted enough to know a couple of the other players, but I don't know many, and I don't know how to get in touch with them. With Jackson dead, I'll have to try to make contact with a man named Bishop Jacobs. He was the man Jackson reported to. If J.P. will vouch for me and for you, Daniel, it will go a long way with Bishop and might just ease our transition into a new cell. If he doesn't, well, that could spell the end of this undercover assignment." She took another drink of her hot chocolate. "Let me start at the beginning. The group I've infiltrated is called the Heritage Guard. It started back in the 1980s up in Virginia and was basically formed as an anti-government group that created its own regional militia and recruited local families. The members thrive on conspiracy theories, and believe they are fighting to save America from a government that is too big, mismanaged and destroying the freedom of the common citizen. They're violent extremists, and they set out a plan to gradually gain strength and money so they could pursue political power and take their ideals to a larger audience. Members have to take an oath of allegiance, and there are different levels of membership."

"What are the different levels?" Daniel asked.

"I still don't know all the ins and outs," Bethany admitted. "But new recruits are at level one. If I'm still accepted, I'll be moved up to level two now that I participated in the bank robbery. There are six levels, six being the top of the pack. Jackson was a three. Bishop is a four."

"What do you have to do to get moved up to the next level?" Daniel asked.

"The threes have planned and executed jobs like the bank robbery. The fours have committed assassinations of enemies of the Heritage Guard. I have no idea what the fives have done. You can bet it's horrific."

Justin leaned forward. "I can tell you about one of their projects that failed. They had a scheme to devalue the American dollar and cripple the economy back in the 1990s by counterfeiting money. The scheme was detected and several of the key players were arrested before the counterfeit bills were actually introduced into the major market streams. Twelve members of the Heritage Guard were tried and convicted under the Racketeer Influenced and Corrupt Organizations Act. The trial dealt a heavy blow to the Guard, but they slowly grew again. Now, they are a lot more secretive and a lot more careful, hence the new organization and the cells that have developed to safeguard their internal structure."

Bethany put down her cup. "They planned to use the cash they were going to steal from the bank to support their political candidates in upcoming elections. They're convinced that placing Guard members in the government is the only way they can get their ideas accepted across mainstream America, and they only want true believers in office. They will do whatever it takes to advance their agenda, including robbing banks to fund their efforts, causing social upheavals, even murdering the opponents. To them, the ends justify the means, no matter the cost, and they have a lot of true believers in their group who will stop at nothing to get their goals accomplished. They have a big project in the works right now called Operation Battlefield. I know it exists, but I don't know what it is or what it entails, although I do think it has something to do with the elections. I don't even know the dates for when it's planned, but there was a sense of urgency around the discussions the last few times it was mentioned, and that's what I'm trying to stop it from happening. From the little I have been able to discover, I know that a lot of people will get hurt if I can't stop it. I'm trying to figure out the details now."

Daniel rubbed his hands through his hair. "So what's our next move?"

Justin handed him a folder and gave one to Bethany, as well. "We created a background for you that melds with the usual type the Heritage Guard tries to recruit, and we've already changed your personnel file and other documents to match this profile. Memorize it. Bethany's background is also in there so you can become familiar with it. Her undercover name is Hailey Weber. Your story is that you knew each other at the University of Tennessee and even dated a bit but didn't want to give that away during the robbery. Now that a few days have passed, we want J.P. and the rest of the Guard to think that you've rekindled your relationship. They already believe Bethany is a true believer, so it won't be that much of stretch for them to think that she dated one in college. Since they didn't score any cash at the bank, they're going to have to plan something fast to find the money they require somewhere else. You need to find out what they're planning and get them to accept you as a member as soon as possible. We also want to know who the other Heritage Guard members are and any details at all about Operation Battlefield."

Bethany widened her eyes. Slow down. Rewind. They wanted her to pretend that she was dating Daniel? She looked over at Daniel and swallowed. He didn't seem bothered by the idea in the least. In fact, if she had to guess, she'd say the look on his face was somewhere between pleasantly surprised and smug. How in the world was she going to do this and keep her emotional distance from him as she'd planned? It was clear that Justin had no idea what he was asking her to do. She felt like going outside and hyperventilating in private. This was not what she had signed up for! She pinched herself hard on the leg. *Okay. Keep it together.* This wasn't the time or place for a meltdown. She tried to focus on the immediate problem. She needed to help get Daniel accepted into the Heritage Guard. "With J.P. arrested and in the hospital, should Daniel escort me there so we can have a visit?"

"That's what I was thinking. He'll obviously realize something is up because he'll recognize Daniel from the robbery. That will be the perfect opportunity for you to feed him the story about Daniel being dirty and wanting to join the cause." Justin stood, his hands on his hips, his voice serious. "I don't have to tell you how dangerous this mission is. The problem at the bank wasn't just a communication failure. There's more. I think there might be a mole in law enforcement. Someone is dirty somewhere, and the communication breakdown was deliberate."

Bethany leaned back abruptly. "Are you kidding me?" She tossed the folder down on the table. "How can I go back in there if I don't know you have my back?"

"I do have your back," Justin said fervently. "And I'm going to find out who the mole is. But this operation is too important to stop right in the middle. We have to push forward. While you're investigating the Heritage Guard, I'll be investigating at the bureau, and I have contacts at the local level that will be looking into the Chattanooga Police Department. We're going to find the mole. I guarantee it."

"Yeah? Well it wasn't you they were targeting at that bank, was it now?" she said vehemently. She knew he outranked her and she was being insubordinate, but good grief, she had almost lost her life, and now he was telling her that her life was at risk both due to her undercover work and from her own team in law enforcement! This day was going from bad to worse. What other great news did he have to share with her?

"I'm not going to let you down, Bethany, or you either, Daniel." He handed them both cell phones. "Talk to me and each other only. No one else. Got it? These phones are clean and untraceable." He handed them each a set of keys. "Because of the bank job and the risk of a leak, I want you to stay at a different apartment. The address is in your folders. I just set this up this morning. Nobody knows about this place but me at this point. It was a last-minute decision."

She smacked her leg with her hands. "Wait a minute. You want us to stay in the same apartment?"

"Sure. It's got two bedrooms."

"But, sir…"

He straightened and furrowed his brow. It was obvious that he was not enjoying her reaction to his edicts. "Do you have a problem with any of this, Agent Walker?"

She glanced over at Daniel again. He seemed to be intensely studying a rather crooked picture of Ruby Falls that was hanging on the wall, trying to stay out of the fray. She felt a sudden urge to kick him under the table. Hard. But she refrained.

"No, sir."

"That's what I thought. To be on the safe side, don't go back to your old apartments, either one of you. I brought you both bags with cash and a few essentials. Let's start this operation fresh from this point forward and see where it leads us."

"Yes, sir," Bethany responded.

Justin shook both their hands. "I think we're close to the end here. Once you two infiltrate the organization again, I think you'll be able to bring this case to a successful conclusion. Operation Battlefield is close. I can feel it. Keep me informed." He gave them a smile and headed out of the restaurant.

Daniel watched him go, secretly pleased that the situation had created an opportunity for him to spend quality time with Bethany. If nothing else, he would have time to figure out what had gone wrong in their relationship. He might not be able to fix whatever problems had arisen, but at least he would understand what had happened.

He opened his folder, pulled out the sheets inside and started scanning the information about his new persona. They hadn't changed much—just added a few new details and altered a couple of things that made his résumé perfect for a Heritage Guard recruit. He found living a lie much easier than living the truth, and he had been doing just that most of his life anyway. His early days had not been pleasant, and he never revealed that part of himself to anyone. He was pleased to see that according to his new dossier, his childhood and teenage years had actually been improved. Maybe this undercover work would be easier for him than he'd thought. It would be like acting in a play. He folded the sheets and put them in his pocket, then turned to Bethany, who had also been reading the file. She raised her eyebrows a couple of times as she took in the information but otherwise didn't react.

"So are you ready to talk?"

She put down the folder. "About what?"

"About us?"

She raised her eyebrows. "I don't think so, Daniel. Now is really not the right time or the place."

"Really? Then when is the right time? Where is the right place?"

She crossed her arms, making him wonder if he would ever be able to pry the answers out of her. Her body language made it clear that she wasn't interested in having him try, at least not right now.

Suddenly a large explosion shook the building, shattering the glass windows and sending bits of debris throughout the restaurant, covering everything and everyone within. Daniel and Bethany immediately hit the floor, but then stood with their weapons ready once they realized there were no further explosions or any bullets flying. Realization hit them both at the same time.

"Oh, no! Justin!" Bethany cried as they caught sight of his SUV that had exploded in the parking lot.

They secured their weapons and rushed outside. Flames were still licking the metal roof of the vehicle and surrounding area, but it was clear that Justin Harper had been killed. The inside of the car was completely black with soot and melting fabric and damaged material, and the bitter smell of burnt rubber and plastic met Daniel's nostrils. He grabbed his police cell phone and called in the explosion, his eyes surveying the scene as he did so. There were no suspicious people milling about, and there had only been a few customers in the diner, none of which had raised his concern. If he had to guess, the bomb had probably been set to go off when Justin turned the ignition of the vehicle. The bomber was probably long gone.

He looked behind him and noticed Bethany had returned to the restaurant and was helping the customers. It didn't look like anyone was seriously injured. A young married couple who had been closer to the windows both had some cuts on their faces and hands from the flying glass. An older man also had a cut on his left cheek, but the restaurant staff seemed unharmed. The waitress had brought out a first aid kit and Bethany was already cleaning and applying salve and Band-Aids to the worst of the cuts. The Christmas decorations that had brightened the diner only a few minutes ago now seemed to be a haunting and macabre sight among the damage and debris.

A few minutes later, Bethany was back by his side. Her features were grim. "I've called Max Westfield at the FBI and let him know what happened."

Daniel wanted to wipe the fear from her eyes, but he knew it was impossible. "Do you trust him?"

She shook her head. "No, but to be honest, I've been gone for so long that after what Justin told us about the mole, I'm not sure who I can trust at the FBI and who I can't. I've been working on my own for a long time, and Max is my only other real contact. Justin was my lifeline. Now I don't know what to do."

"Who's Justin's boss?"

"A woman named Sandra Duval. I've only met her once. I assume she'll replace Justin at some point now that he's gone."

"Well, we have three options. We can contact her, or we can go straight to the US attorney who prosecuted the Heritage Guard under the RICO statute. Maybe they can help us."

"And option number three?"

"We can contact Captain Murphy, my boss, and bring in the local team."

Bethany paced a few steps back and forth, her arms

tightly wrapped around her stomach. "I have to think about this. *We* have to think about this before we contact anyone. If whoever killed Justin killed him because of this case, they probably also know about me and maybe even you and our connection to the Heritage Guard. We could be next."

Daniel rubbed his hands through his hair. "Or maybe the killer doesn't know about us. Perhaps the mole knew he was being investigated, and he killed Justin to stop the investigation. He might know Justin had someone trying to infiltrate the Guard, but the mole might not know that anyone was successful, or that you are the one who actually became a member of the Guard. There's no telling what the mole knows or doesn't know at this point. There are a hundred possibilities. We need more information before we talk to anyone else."

He heard a siren approaching from the distance and he gently grasped Bethany's shoulders. "You need to disappear. I'm the cop that called this in, so they'll expect me to be here, but I don't want you anywhere near this place. I'll tell them Justin had some questions about the robbery, we talked and then the SUV exploded when he left. We'll meet up in a couple of hours at the hospital and see J.P., okay?"

"Okay. Call me on the new cell if there are any developments."

He leaned forward and gave her a quick kiss on the forehead, and he was surprised when she didn't protest before she turned and disappeared into the gathering crowd.

Their handler was dead. He had declared that there was a mole and that he was in the process of investigating that mole, and then he had subsequently been murdered. The implications of what had happened were just starting to sink into Daniel's thoughts.

The Heritage Guard had to have infiltrated law enforcement, but was the mole in the FBI, or was he in the local police office where Daniel worked? Who did they report to now? Who could they trust? There were too many questions, and not nearly enough answers.

NINE

"Hailey!" The smile that greeted her instantly disappeared when J.P. saw that Daniel accompanied her. "What's he doing here?" He pulled against the cuffs that had him shackled to the hospital bed as if he could somehow get farther away from the dreaded man by doing so, his expression hostile as he watched Daniel enter his room.

Bethany nodded at Daniel, hoping he would get the message and stay near the door. He would still be able to hear from that position, but it would give J.P. the illusion of privacy. Daniel got the silent message and leaned against the door frame as she went up to J.P.'s side.

"He's with me, J.P."

"Why? And why are you here? You betrayed me. And I've been hearing rumors. Bad rumors about what happened to the rest of the team."

Bethany pulled up a chair. "Look, I know you're not happy about being arrested, but you're alive. You would have died from your wounds if I hadn't acted.

That's a fact that was confirmed by the EMT at the scene. Surely, they've told you that here at the hospital, as well. You were going into shock because you had lost so much blood." She looked him directly in the eye. "You're too important to the cause, J.P. We can't afford to lose you."

The man was nothing if not prideful. He looked like he still wanted to argue with her, but at the same time, he seemed pleased with her compliment. He stole a look at Daniel, then lowered his voice. "Tell me what happened after I got pulled out of there. I need details. Nobody is telling me much."

"It's bad, J.P."

"I know Jackson is dead."

Bethany nodded soberly. "Yes. They killed Terrell and John too. It was awful. So you see, if you had stayed, you would probably have died regardless."

J.P. shook his head, his expression somewhere between sorrow and anger. His brow was knit together, and his frown put deep creases in his face. "Tell me what happened. Don't leave out a thing."

She glanced up at Daniel, and could tell he was listening, but to his credit, he was looking into the hallway as if he still couldn't hear their conversation. She turned her attention back to J.P. "Well, Daniel Morley, the guy I'm with, he's actually a cop. But he's not just any cop. Turns out, I know him. He and I used to date when we were in college."

J.P. turned and quickly looked over at Daniel, who was still appearing to ignore them. "Yeah? I thought you seemed to be protecting him a bit too much."

She ignored that. "I didn't know he was a cop at the time. We hadn't seen each other in a few years and we hadn't kept in touch. I didn't know what he ended up doing for a living. Anyway, after you left, I, ah, well, I had to rough him up a little to keep him quiet and afterward, Terrell made me take him into the bathroom to clean him up. While we were back there, local law enforcement decided to raid the bank. They came in through the ceiling in full riot gear and shot and killed the rest of the team in a matter of seconds. It turns out Daniel still has feelings for me, and he didn't want me to get killed like the others, or even arrested. He helped me hide the gun and mask, and I walked out with the rest of the hostages."

J.P. narrowed his eyes. "Why would he do that? You just said he's a cop, right? Why didn't he just arrest you and turn you over?"

She leaned in closer, her voice quiet. "While we were back in the bathroom, I was able to talk to him again, you know, really talk. He's a true believer too, J.P. He agrees with the Guard's manifesto. When I explained to him why we were at the bank and what we were trying to do, he said he wanted to help."

"Was he a true believer back when you were dating before?"

She shrugged. "Not as much as he is now. I mean, we wouldn't have dated if we hadn't shared some of the same beliefs, but now, well, he's had some setbacks."

J.P. raised his eyebrow. "Setbacks?"

Bethany smiled inwardly. The FBI had created a good backstory for Daniel. Now they only had to sell it. "Turns out his father lost his construction business due to the government unfairly giving out contracts. It had been in the family for three generations. His father lost everything. I'm telling you, he used to be a straight arrow, but he's not anymore. He's ready to fight for the cause."

Bethany watched J.P. carefully, trying to gauge if he was believing her story. He seemed to be mulling it over in his mind, but he had always been a hothead and difficult for her to read. Why couldn't it have been Terrell who had survived? At least she had always had a laidback camaraderie with Terrell that made it easy to talk to him. J.P. was a young, impetuous firebrand. Working with him made her nervous, but she didn't have any choice. J.P. had survived, and J.P. was the one she had to deal with.

"Do you trust him?"

"I don't know," she said softly, trying to make it seem like she was hiding the answers from Daniel's listening ears. She didn't think J.P. would buy it if she joined forces with a cop in a matter of a couple of days, so she wanted to introduce the idea to him gradually. Without Justin to guide her, she was making this all up as she went along. "I haven't been around him in a very long time. I know he's passionate about what he believes. He always has been, and now he's even more so. We've started dating again, so we'll see what happens. I do know I'm not in jail. That's a pretty good start. He helped me out at the bank, and that's a fact. Sometimes actions speak louder than words."

J.P. nodded and took another look at Daniel as if

he were considering Bethany's opinion. "Yeah, talk to him a lot and see if you can see if he really is a true believer. If he is, we could use a cop on the inside."

"That's exactly what I was thinking." She leaned close again. "Look, J.P., I don't know what to do next. Jackson was my leader, and I don't know anybody else but you from the Guard. I mean, I've seen some faces here and there, and I know a few names, like that guy Bishop Jacobs, but I really don't know how to contact anyone now that Jackson's gone. How do I get reconnected? I'm feeling a little lost right now and I need your help."

He raised his eyebrows as if considering her words. He studied her face for a moment as if judging her veracity, then finally seemed to make a decision. "Go to the dry cleaners on Fifth and Stadium downtown. Tell them you want to sign up for the monthly special. Tell them J.P. sent you. Then leave your name and cell phone number. Someone will contact you."

"That's it?"

"That's it."

"How long will it take?"

J.P. frowned. "Are you in some sort of hurry?"

She blew out a breath. "Of course not. But I want them to pay for what they did to Jackson and the rest of the team. That was my family. They killed *our* family. I want to make them pay. Don't you?"

J.P. seemed satisfied. He grinned at her. "Don't worry. We've got something bigger coming down the pike. They'll pay for what they did at that bank alright."

She grabbed his arm and gave it a squeeze, thinking

it was prudent not to push him for more right now. She didn't want him to get suspicious in any way. "Thanks, J.P. You're the best." She leaned back. "So are you going to be okay?"

"I've been arraigned and have a public defender. They want to do a deal but I won't rat on our friends. And I've got plenty of friends on the inside. I'll be safe enough."

"How's your health? Did that bullet do any serious damage?"

"No worries there. In a month or two, I'll be playing basketball in the jail yard, reading about you and the glory of the Guard."

"You can count on it." She patted his hand and stood. Then she joined Daniel who nodded at J.P. before they left the hospital. J.P. would be reading about the Guard in the news alright, but if she had anything to say about it, it would be because the whole lot of them had been arrested and thrown in prison.

Daniel and Bethany rode in silence to a nearby grocery store, and even said very little as they purchased a few items. Bethany called Max Westfield on her burner phone and they discussed Justin's death in more detail. She told him about their visit with J.P. Max was very supportive and promised he would contact her again once a new supervising agent was assigned. For now, he told her that she and Daniel should lay low until Justin's murderer was found. Bethany listened, but Daniel doubted she had any plans to lay low.

After navigating to their new apartment, they

made it up the stairs and entered the living room of the second-story unit. Daniel could tell that the loss of Justin Harper and dealing with J.P. at the hospital were all weighing heavily on Bethany, and he wished she weren't quite so independent and would let him ease some of her burden. She had always wanted to handle everything by herself, which at times had been a source of contention between the two of them. Since they were no longer a couple, he hoped she would at least allow him to offer some friendship and support, but so far, her silence seemed to be sending him only one message: *Stay away, I don't need you.* How did he bridge that gap? He wasn't sure, but he wasn't going to give up either. He still had feelings for her. Strong feelings. She was worth fighting for, and he was going to do whatever it took to show her that she could love him and maintain her independence at the same time. He had made a mess of it the first time, but God had granted him a second chance, and this time, he was going to get it right. Finding Bethany and getting to spend quality time with her was an answer to his prayers.

Daniel threw his duffel bag carelessly on the couch and made his way to the kitchen with the groceries while Bethany did a sweep of the bedrooms.

"See any problems?" he asked as he put the cold groceries into the refrigerator.

"No. It's your basic apartment layout. The bedrooms are almost identical. You can have your pick. Each has a bath and balcony."

She had never been one of those females that fussed over fluff and nonsense. She had never wanted jewelry or flowers as presents either. Her idea of the perfect gift was always something practical that she would use on a regular basis. He liked that about her, but it also made it hard to shop for her for Christmas and birthdays. Funny, but he had forgotten that detail about her until just this moment. He offered her a smile and a bottled water. "Want something to drink?"

"Not really." She yawned and stretched. "Thanks anyway."

He could see the weariness in her face and the haggard expression in her eyes. He wanted to just hold her and lend her some of his strength, but he could tell from the standoffish way she held herself that she wouldn't accept his overture, and wouldn't appreciate the offer either. She was in her independent mode again, and if he were correct in his guess, she was about to call it a day and disappear into her room and lock the door.

He tried something else, hoping it would keep her in his presence and communicating with him for little bit longer. "I got you a surprise."

She raised an eyebrow. "Oh, really?" She tried to look into the brown grocery bag he was protectively guarding but he folded down the top and pulled it out of her reach. "No, ma'am. Make yourself comfortable on the couch and I'll bring it over in a minute or two."

She playfully narrowed her eyes. "You know I have a gun, right, and that I'm trained in how to use it?" she said, her voice full of mirth.

He smiled, relieved that she was willing to play along. "Don't forget, missy, I've got a gun myself. And

I've logged a few hours at the firing range too. Trust me. Have a seat and you won't regret it."

She watched him for a moment or two before finally heading to the couch. He moved out of her line of vision, prepared the surprise and called out to her before he headed back into the living room. "Close your eyes."

"Really?"

"Really! Come on now. Play fair."

"Okay, fine," she said in mock exasperation. She closed her eyes.

He joined her on the couch and held a bowl up a few inches under her nose. "Okay, you can open them," he said softly.

She opened her eyes, and smiled in delight when she saw the bowl with triple-chocolate ice cream that was swimming in chocolate syrup. Underneath the ice cream was a warm brownie with nuts that Daniel had heated in the microwave. It was a chocolate lover's dream, and he knew it had been her favorite dessert since middle school. He was even wearing a red Santa's hat to help celebrate the season.

She sighed. "You remembered." She grabbed the bowl from him and eagerly took a bite.

"Of course, I remembered," Daniel laughed. "There aren't many people who can eat that much chocolate in one sitting without overdosing and being rushed to the hospital. It's kinda hard to forget." He took a bite of his own ice cream, which had half the amount of chocolate syrup on it and no brownie, and leaned back on the couch. Even though the day had been difficult and demanding, he was enjoying the camaraderie they had shared through the sorrow, pain and even exhilaration at getting what they needed from J.P. at the hospital. He enjoyed working with her, but more than that—he enjoyed having her back in his life.

"So how is your family?"

The question she asked seemed innocent enough, yet it caused a tightening in his stomach that he hadn't expected. He rarely talked about his family with anyone. He shifted. Okay, he never talked about his family. Still, he couldn't expect her not to ask. He shrugged as if the question didn't bother him. "Mom is still living out west. Not much has changed. My brother is in Miami."

"Have you heard from either of them lately?"

"No." He didn't elaborate, and he changed the subject. "What about you? How are your parents?"

She looked him in the eyes and he was aware that *she* knew there was more to the story, but she didn't challenge him on his answer. Instead, she sighed and took another bite, just watching him. Her look told him she was disappointed in him, but there was no surprise in her features. Finally, she shrugged and answered his question, allowing him to change the subject. "They're living the retired life down in Tallahassee. They're happy between their church family and their Florida State Seminoles women's basketball games. There's always something to keep them hopping. They even started going to the theater at FSU, although Dad still doesn't love the musicals, even though he tolerates them for Mom's sake. They'll be Seminole fans till they drop I suspect."

"Have they seen any good plays?"

"They mentioned *Arsenic and Old Lace* and *The Music Man*, and they were pretty excited to see *The Phantom of the Opera* on the playbill for next year's opener. That's Mom's favorite show ever. She can't get enough of the music."

He smiled, remembering Bethany's mom was a theater buff and drummer in her own right. "Didn't she see *Phantom* on Broadway?"

Bethany laughed. "Yeah, twice, and she saw it in Las Vegas too. She says the music still gives her goosebumps when she hears it live. She just loves it." She smiled, reminiscing. "You know, the lady rarely spends a dollar on herself, but when it comes to a good theater production, she'll actually splurge and buy front row tickets just to enjoy the experience. She took a few of the kids to New York recently and got front row seats to *Les Misérables*. They all said it was amazing. They could actually make eye contact with the actors." She finished her dessert and took the bowl to the kitchen and rinsed it, then passed him again on her way to her bedroom.

"I'm done in. See you in the morning?"

He nodded, glad the dessert had given them an opportunity to talk about something besides work and the Heritage Guard. "Sure. 8:00 a.m.?"

"Sounds good."

He was glad that she was willing to share about her family, but why did she seem so disappointed that he didn't want to talk about his? That was all the past, and he didn't understand her need or desire to dig through the remnants of where he had come from. It was over and done with, yet she still asked those same questions. He wanted to focus on the here and now. He didn't want to live in the past. He certainly didn't want to dredge up old memories or talk about people who no longer had a place in his life.

His new cell phone vibrated and he pulled it out and looked at the screen. It was the phone Justin had given him right before he was murdered and so far, he hadn't received a single call on the line. Justin had told them to trust no one. Should he answer? He didn't recognize the number. He was tempted to ignore the call. It vibrated again and again in his hand. He had meant to turn it off and take the battery out once Justin had been killed, or at a minimum discuss it with Bethany before he acted, but it had simply slipped his mind. Could someone locate them now that his phone had been called? Had he just jeopardized their mission? After all, it was a clean phone from the FBI, and as far as he knew, only Justin, Bethany and he knew the number. It was probably a wrong number, but even so, he was incredibly curious about who was on the other end of the line. The phone vibrated again, but he didn't answer. Instead, he wrote down the number that was calling on a slip of paper, then made a mental note to call it in tomorrow to his contact at the office to run a trace on the number. Could it be Justin's killer? Or someone from the Guard? Time would tell. He turned off the phone and removed the battery just in case.

TEN

Bethany looked to the left and right, then crossed Stadium Street and entered the dry cleaners on the corner. It was a busy store and there were three customers in line ahead of her. She pulled out a brochure from a display on the counter and perused it as she waited, looking up from time to time. There was nothing out of the ordinary about the store to suggest it was anything but a dry cleaners. Racks of clothing in dry-cleaning bags were behind the counter and the shop smelled of cleaning fluids and bleach. Posters on the walls advertised a variety of prices and deals available to special customers, as well as special ticket discounts for tourists that wanted to visit Ruby Falls or the Tennessee Aquarium. A small Christmas tree was also standing in the corner, decorated tastefully in red-and-green glass balls of various shapes and designs. Underneath the tree were several wrapped packages that added to the festive air.

A holiday tune played on the sound system and Bethany sang along to the Christmas carol. When it was her turn, she approached the young man at the register. He was blond with blue eyes and a ready smile. "May I help you?"

She smiled back. "Yes, I'd like to sign up for the monthly special."

The man looked a bit confused. "Monthly special?"

Bethany nodded. "Ah, yes. My friend J.P. gets all of his clothes dry-cleaned here. He told me about the monthly special for your best customers, but said I needed to sign up to get the discount. He recommended that I come in here."

The man pushed a pad across the counter. "I'll have to ask the manager if we're still offering that deal. Please write down your name and cell phone number, and he'll call you back as soon as he gets a chance to check on the latest specials. Will that work?"

She shrugged. "Sounds perfect to me. I'm not in a rush. I'm more interested in quality than speed."

"Well, we just might be able to help you then." He pulled the pad back over to himself after she had finished writing, removed the top sheet with her information and pocketed the paper. "We'll be in touch."

"Thanks."

She left and returned to Daniel, who was waiting across the street for her. It was a bit chilly and she pulled her jacket closer as she approached. "See anything?"

Daniel shook his head. "Nobody followed you, and I didn't see any suspicious people milling about, but my money is on surveillance cameras. I see three things that could be cameras, and they're making surveillance equipment so small these days, there could be even more. There's no telling for sure." Bethany noticed a spark in his eye, but when he took her in his arms and leaned forward to kiss her, she pulled back, unsure. "What are you doing?"

He gave her a smile and touched her nose affectionately. "We're supposed to be dating, remember? We've rekindled a lost love and are sharing an apartment? If anyone from the Guard is watching us, you can bet they have someone stationed near this dry-cleaning place, and I'm sure they've got their eyes on us right now."

He made a valid point. She laughed, hoping to cover up her gaff in case he was right. She had to sell this romance between them, whether she felt it or not. "You're right. I'm sorry." She drew her hand down his face in a gesture of intimacy, then pulled him into an embrace. She found herself enjoying the contact more than she thought she would, yet still she felt herself awkwardly tighten up in his embrace. Daniel was warm and his strength made her feel safe and secure, but letting Daniel go and moving on with her life had been two of the hardest things she'd ever done. She didn't want to open herself up to that kind of hurt again. Letting him be a part of this mission and pretending they were a couple were both going to be harder than she'd ever imagined.

"Is it really that difficult to let me help you?"

She pulled back, surprised at his question and also frustrated that he had hit the nail on the head. Instead of admitting her own issues, she went on the offensive. "I can't believe you're asking me that. I should be asking you that question."

He took her hand and they started walking down the street as if they were carefree lovers but inside, her stomach was in knots. She had been avoiding this conversation with Daniel ever since she had first seen him at the bank, but maybe it was time they hashed it out. If they weren't going to be able to work together, they needed to know it now before the Guard drew her into the new cell and Daniel became even more deeply entrenched in his role in this undercover assignment.

"Do you know why I never set the date to walk down the aisle with you?" she asked quietly.

His grip tightened on her fingers, but that was the only sign that he was affected by her question. He was apparently quite aware that they needed to maintain appearances in case their performance was being watched by the Guard, even as they got farther and farther away from the dry cleaners.

"No, I still don't understand. I thought we were in love."

She smiled at him. "There are so many things I love about you, Daniel. I love that you remembered my favorite dessert. I love the way you are considerate and kind to others. I love your giving heart." She gave him a playful nudge as they walked and he laughed. "And I think you are the most handsome man I have ever met in my entire life. You have the most amazing shoulders…and you look absolutely fantastic in a Santa's hat."

He laughed with her but stopped when he noticed the look on her face. "Why do I sense a big *but* coming my way?"

She shrugged. "Do you remember last night when I shared a few details about my family?"

"Sure. I enjoy hearing about them."

"Well, last night was a perfect example. When we talk, Daniel, it's always me sharing, never you. I can't marry you because I don't even think I know who the real Daniel is. You rarely share details about yourself. You don't tell me about your past, and I'm left guessing about who you really are inside."

He stopped and looked her in the eye. "That's not true. I've shared more of myself with you than with anyone."

She met his eye, but then dropped his hand and kept walking. He paused a moment, but then followed her, taking her hand again. "That might be true, but I still don't really know you, Daniel. Even after we dated for a year. Even after you asked me to marry you."

"We talked all the time. I remember having long conversations."

"I talked. I told you about myself and my family. And don't get me wrong, you were a good listener. But when you talked, it was about your job or maybe current events. We'd talk about anything and everything *but* you. There was never anything personal in the conversation. You never told me about your past and where you came from. I don't really know you. I don't even know what you feel or what you think. I never have."

"Yes, you do. You know me better than anyone. The rest are just details. They don't matter. What you see here and now, that's who I am today. I don't want to live in the past. I didn't have a great childhood, and there's no reason to relive it by bringing it up."

They turned down a different street, and she was glad for the diversion of walking so they could discuss this difficult topic. She couldn't imagine sitting on a couch and having this conversation. She was sure he would have shut her down after the first sentence if they'd been in the apartment trying to sort this out. There was something good about walking and talking that helped get the words out. She took a deep breath and pushed on. It was time to broach the subject that had been eating at her the longest. "You told me your mother lives out west."

Once again, she felt his hand tighten on her own. She could tell this conversation was difficult for him, yet, they still needed to talk about this elephant in the room if they were going to work together or ever have anything more. "That's a lie, Daniel, or at least a huge omission."

He raised an eyebrow, and for the first time, she saw a look of fear cross his face. "What do you mean?"

"I work in law enforcement, remember? I did some research and tracked her down. Your mom is in prison out in Texas for drug possession. She's been incarcerated for over ten years. You've never mentioned that. In fact, you've never told me anything about her. And apparently, you have an older brother. Don't you think you've left out a few of the important details?"

He didn't speak for a long time. When he finally did, his voice was rough and there was anger in its depths. "What do you want to hear? That my dad abandoned us when I was five and my mom's drugs were more important to her than I ever was? It didn't take me long to figure out I needed to make myself scarce whenever she was using. I got pretty good at disappearing. Is that what you want to hear? Or maybe you want to know about how my older brother used to beat me up whenever he felt like it? Or about how I spent my evenings hiding outside under the car, or went for days without eating a decent meal? Is that what you want to know about?"

Bethany stopped and tried to pull him close, but this time, Daniel was the one that reeled back. "I don't want pity. That's a big reason why I don't talk about it. I'm not that scared little boy anymore. I grew up quickly and I learned how to take care of myself. But I did a lot of things that I'm not proud of too. I had to survive. And survival meant stealing sometimes so I could eat, and some things that were a lot worse. I had to do a lot of terrible things. Is that what you want to hear? Is this what you want to talk about?" His voice was angry and when she reached for him again, he put up his hands and walked away from her. She followed a short distance behind, and for almost two blocks, they walked in silence.

Finally, he stopped and ran his fingers through his hair. He turned to face her, but he wouldn't look at her directly. "I can't believe I just told you that," he said, his voice soft. "I've never told anybody that."

She touched his chin and raised his head so she could see his eyes. He had such beautiful eyes. "I'm really glad you did, because that's who you are. I want to know you, all of you, the good, the bad and the ugly. I am sorry that happened to you, Daniel, but I don't want to hear the stories so I can pity you. I want to hear so I can get to know you better. So I know that you trust me enough to tell me. So I can know the real you. You're an incredible person, Daniel. You must have overcome some amazing hurdles in your life to become so successful. I want to know how you did it. I want to get to know you in here." She touched his chest.

He studied her for a moment or two, then took her hand again and started walking. "And if I don't want to tell you?"

Bethany considered his words. Could they have a relationship without trust? Maybe for a while. But months from now, that lack of trust would eat at her, just as it had when she had found out the truth about his mother and her prison sentence. She had read that law enforcement file and it had been like someone had stuck a knife in her gut. She'd had a serious boyfriend before who cheated on her and ended up humiliating her in front of her friends and coworkers. She had trusted him and vowed to never make the same mistake again. Daniel was a different man, and she could never imagine him cheating on her, but trust was a vital part of any relationship. Without it, she would rather be alone and take her chances on her own.

"Then I guess friendship will have to be enough, Daniel. For both of us. I don't want to force you to do anything you don't want to do. That's not what I'm about, and it's obvious that you don't want to give more than you've already given. That's fair. It's your life and it's your choice. You don't have to give more. I know we're pretending to be more for this job, but I'm glad we were able to talk and clear the air. Now we know where we stand. We'll play this game for the Heritage Guard assignment, but once this is over, we'll go our separate ways, okay?" She stopped walking, and when he turned to face her, she reached up on tiptoe and gave him a quick kiss on the lips. "But now we'll part friends, okay?"

He looked like he was about to argue with her, but then her cell phone rang, and she answered it on the second ring. "Hello?"

"Did you make up with your boyfriend?"

She smiled and looked around, completely in her role for whomever was watching from the Guard. "Making up is always the best part. Where are you?"

"Nearby."

"Who am I talking to?" Bethany knew it had to be someone associated with the Guard, because the only person she had given this phone number to was the man at the dry cleaners.

"We've met before, but it was quite a while ago. My name is Bishop Jacobs. You were part of Jackson's team."

"That's right."

"I've heard you can get things."

"That's also right," she agreed.

"I have some friends I'd like for you to meet," Bishop stated, his tone friendly yet businesslike.

"I'm all for that. When and where?"

"Two hours. Coolidge Park. By the carousel."

"How will I recognize these new friends?"

"You don't need to worry. We'll recognize you," Bishop stated, matter-of-factly.

"Alright then. I'll be there," Bethany agreed.

"Don't bring your boyfriend."

"Why not? He wants to join up."

"We might let him. We might be able to use someone with his particular skill set. But we're still checking him out. Leave him at home, understand?"

She shrugged as if it didn't matter. "Whatever. It's your show."

"Yes, it is," Bishop agreed. "And it's going to be fabulous."

ELEVEN

The Dentzel carousel in Coolidge Park was a true work of art. Daniel admired the hand-carved animals and ornate decorations between the gold leaf benches through the binoculars as he kept an eye on Bethany waiting for the Guard contact to arrive. The park had also been decorated for Christmas, and bright red ribbons were on every post between hanging swaths of garland intertwined with strings of cranberries and popcorn. Hand-drawn pictures of traditional Christmas designs like reindeer, nativity scenes and snowflakes were posted on some of the walls, as well as a sign stating the art was donated by a local elementary school's fifth grade class. Daniel was tempted to put down a couple of dollars and take Bethany on a ride once this entire episode was over, but the seriousness of the job at hand kept his mind off of his surroundings and focused on the job at hand.

Their discussion this morning had been like pouring salt on open wounds, and he still couldn't believe that he had blurted out so much about himself. He and his older brother didn't talk. They didn't have a relationship worth mentioning.

He *never* talked about his mother.

It was a rule he had lived by since he had closed that chapter of his life when she was arrested. He had watched her being cuffed and led away on that fateful day, and in his mind, that was the end of their relationship. He hadn't wanted to think about her or even know what was happening in her life since the police took her away. He was done. He had moved on. If he never saw either one of them again for the rest of his life, that would be okay with him. Yet, he had shared bits and pieces of his past with Bethany this morning and it had been oddly cathartic. Still, he had no desire to go any further with the discussion, and he tried to put it from his mind.

Why was Bethany so set on knowing his past? The question ate at him as he used the binoculars to scan the area. He saw two other men surveilling the area around the carousel that were probably with the Guard. He texted Bethany about them, using a special code they had devised so no one would understand their messages if either of the phones were confiscated. She texted back and let him know that she had seen them too, and he leaned back against the fence, once again surveying the area through the binoculars. Both men were obviously not there for the carousel. He kept watching.

He thought back over the year that he and Bethany had dated, and sorted through as many of the conversations they'd had as he could remember. He grudgingly had to admit that she had a point. He *hadn't* told her much about himself. But why did it matter? She had seen that he was a caring and good person, right? They had spent a great deal of time together, and she had learned a lot about his personality. He knew her last boyfriend had been a real prince and had publicly cheated on her. Surely, she knew he wasn't cut from that cloth. Wasn't that enough? He grimaced. Apparently, it wasn't. Especially if her "parting as friends" comment was anything to go by. Now he was well and truly stuck in a quandary. He didn't want to talk about his past, and he didn't want to lose Bethany either.

"Freeze, buddy."

Daniel heard the words seconds before he felt the metal of the gun barrel against his side. He kicked himself mentally. He had been so engrossed in his thoughts that he hadn't even noticed that the two men had snuck up on him. He felt like an idiot. He did as he was told as one man wearing a Rays baseball cap took Daniel's gun out of his waistband, while a man on his left wearing a red flannel shirt took his binoculars and his cell phone, then patted him down. Both men were blond and looked to be in their thirties. They were well built and both gave off a self-assured and aggressive vibe. They could have been brothers, with similar features, including high cheekbones and deep-set hazel eyes.

"Look," the one Daniel nicknamed Flannel said lightly, nudging his partner as he found Daniel's badge and pulled it out of his pocket and examined it. "Our friend here is a cop."

"Is there a problem?" Daniel asked in a nonchalant voice. He hoped they were Guard members but didn't want to assume anything. He chose not to challenge them and thought a non-aggressive response was the best way to respond. It made sense that the Guard would want to have people on the perimeter of the meeting as well; he just thought that he had been far enough back that he wouldn't draw their attention. He had been wrong. If he were also wrong about who they were and he had just let common criminals get the jump on him and take his gun, he was in a great deal of trouble. In either case, he was on high alert and his muscles were tensed and ready for action at the slightest provocation.

"Are you on the job or off?" the Rays fan asked, pushing the gun a little harder against his ribs.

"I'm looking out for a friend."

The man got even closer and spoke in a low tone, yet the threat in his tone was obvious. "You didn't answer my question, *friend*. And I'm not fond of repeating myself."

Daniel gritted his teeth. "And I'm not fond of getting threatened. A cop is always on the job, but to answer your question more specifically, I'm not here representing the police department today. I'm here helping out a friend."

Flannel motioned with his hand. "Helping out how? I don't see anyone but you. Maybe you're some kind of criminal just casing the place. Maybe that isn't even a real badge."

"It's real alright."

Flannel laughed. "You really don't like answering questions directly, do you?"

The Rays fan took a step back and looked more carefully at Daniel's expression. When he finally spoke again, his voice was thoughtful. "I'm pretty sure you were told to stay home."

Daniel nodded, but inwardly relaxed a measure. The man's words reassured him that they were with the Guard and knew about Bethany's meeting. He was still on high alert however. He didn't know what to expect, but his undercover mission to infiltrate this group had officially begun. "You're right, but it's hard to stay back when you care about someone. I was out of the way if you wanted to meet with her in private. I'm not eavesdropping on any personal conversations. I just wanted to verify that she was safe."

"You didn't trust us?" Flannel scoffed. The Rays fan shot him a look that shut him up. It was clear that he was the one in charge and he didn't want any superfluous conversations.

Daniel shrugged. "I don't trust blindly. Do you? I don't even know you. Yet."

The Rays fan stepped closer again and this time there was something dark and threatening in his eyes. "We don't trust people who don't follow orders." He looked Daniel up and down as if taking his measure. "We also don't trust cops." He handed Daniel back his badge, binoculars and phone, but stowed Daniel's gun in his own waistband and covered it with his shirt. Then he pushed Daniel forward. "Head toward the carousel. Keep your hands where I can see them."

Daniel obeyed, but stayed on alert. "I'll need my gun back after this meeting."

"You'll get it back when I'm good and ready to give it back. Not before. Now keep walking."

They walked in silence for a few minutes, but then Daniel said, "Not all cops are the same you know. We don't all live by the same code."

"How do you figure?" Flannel asked.

"I believe a man should earn what he gets and get what he earns. There are no free rides in this world. But not everyone in law enforcement agrees with me." When he got no response, he pushed on, knowing he had to play a role, even though he didn't necessarily agree inside with everything he would be saying and doing while trying to infiltrate the Heritage Guard. "My point is, you might actually trust a cop if you knew the right cop. Some of us agree with what you're trying to accomplish." He could tell that they were thinking about his words, so he didn't push. The key to being accepted might also be to keep his mouth shut for the most part and just listen and learn. The FBI had created a very credible background story for him, and if he said a bit here and there that supported it and then just shut up and did what was asked of him, he might be accepted into the Heritage Guard without even a raised eyebrow.

Daniel said a prayer for Bethany's safety since he was no longer able to keep an eye on her. Yet, he was cognizant of the fact that she had already been undercover with this group for over a year, so she was probably safer than he was in his current situation. He followed Flannel into a building that was behind the carousel, quite aware that the Rays fan was still armed and following him from behind.

The room they entered was bare except for a long table and six folding chairs. There were no windows, and the room only had one door in or out. It was probably normally used for storage and was dusty and smelled like stale cleaning supplies and paper goods. The Rays fan motioned toward one of the chairs.

"Sit."

Daniel picked the chair farthest from the door so he could be the first to see anyone coming or going from the room. He eased himself down, keeping an eye on Flannel and the Rays fan as he did so. Both of the men stationed themselves by the door, almost like sentries. He wasn't sure why he had been brought here, and neither man seemed ready to volunteer any information. After about ten minutes of waiting, impatience finally got the best of him.

"We waiting for someone?" Daniel asked.

"Yeah. Just hang tight," Flannel answered.

Suddenly, the door opened and a bull of a man barreled in and tackled Daniel, even though he was still sitting in the chair. Both men ended up on the floor and the chair Daniel had been sitting in went flying. It was all Daniel could do to keep from getting his nose bashed against the floor again as both men landed hard on the concrete. Daniel struggled to free his arms and once he did, he hit the aggressor's head against the wall as they rolled and wrestled for supremacy. Daniel knocked the man hard in the chin with his elbow and the attacker loosened his grip just enough so Daniel was able to roll him over, gain the upper hand and end up on top. He straddled the larger man and hit him hard in the mouth, drawing blood with the blow. A second punch drew blood from the man's nose, but before he could throw a third, Flannel and the Rays fan joined the fray and pulled the two apart. The one Daniel had nicknamed "the Bull" spat blood on the floor and tried to pull away, his face contorted by the mess Daniel had made with his fists.

"Filthy cop!" the Bull roared. "Because of you, my cousin is dead!" He tried again to pull loose from the Rays fan but the bigger man held him fast.

"I don't know your cousin, and I don't know you," Daniel answered, also jerking against Flannel's grip. He'd had enough of these guys. Maybe they would respect him more if he showed them some fire, but either way, he was done getting attacked without provocation. He was going to defend himself. He felt blood trickling down his face and realized he hadn't successfully protected his nose after all. The rush of adrenaline kept him from feeling the pain for now, but he was sure his face would start throbbing again once this episode was over. The way his week was going, he figured his nose would never heal normally again.

"So tell me about your boyfriend," Bishop said as he leaned back and crossed his legs. His phone beeped and he looked at the screen, then silenced it and put it in his pocket. Bishop and Bethany were alone in the room, sitting across a rickety table from each other in a small building not far from the carousel. Another man had frisked her and taken her cell phone and sidearm when she was brought in. He gave both items to Bishop, then slipped outside and was probably guarding the door.

Bethany shrugged. "His name is Daniel Morley. We dated a bit in college, then went our own ways. I ran across him again during the bank robbery. He saved my life."

"He's a cop?" Bishop asked.

Bethany smiled. She was having trouble reading Bishop, but she could tell he already knew the answer to the question before he even asked. She had met him a couple of times before, but didn't really know him, or what role he played in the organization beyond the basics. Justin had started to dig into his background, but they still knew little besides the fact that he owned and operated a mid-size rental car company. She did know he was powerful within the Guard, and she needed him to trust her if her mission was going to be a success. He was a distinguished looking man in his early fifties, with weathered skin and dark intelligent eyes. He had shortly cropped dark hair that was just starting to gray and a silver mustache. She could tell by his demeanor that he was used to being in charge and not having his orders questioned. Now he seemed to be testing her, but she wasn't sure what he was looking for. The direct approach always seemed to work best for her. She tried it now. "Let's quit playing games, Mr. Jacobs. I'm sure you already know his full history and have done a thorough background check. Is there something specific you want to know?"

"Fair enough," Bishop answered. "Let's cut to the

chase. I want to know why he came with you today when I specifically told you not to bring him."

She raised an eyebrow and tried to act calm and collected, even though her heart was beating through her chest. If they had found Daniel in the park, then he was probably in danger. They'd thought if he stayed far enough back, he wouldn't be seen by any of the Guard. Obviously, they had been wrong. Was he hurt? Had their mistake jeopardized the mission? Questions fluttered across her mind, along with a healthy dose of fear. Still, she kept her emotions well below the surface and answered in a nonchalant voice. "He wasn't close enough to get in the way," she said quietly. "But since I almost got killed at the bank just a couple of days ago, Daniel was worried about my safety."

"We take care of our own. You should know that."

"I do," Bethany answered. "But I just lost my entire team, and I still don't know why. Something went terribly wrong at the bank, and until I know the reasons for their deaths, I'm being extra cautious, and so is he."

"Cautious is good," Bishop agreed. He steepled his fingers as he considered her words. "Defiance is not. I'm inclined to assign you to a new team, but I need to know that you are still loyal to the Guard. I need to know that you will follow orders in the future without question."

Bethany tightened her fists. "The Guard is my family. I lost everything and everyone I cared about in that bank job. I'm still loyal, but now I'm also on fire for the cause even more than before. The police killed my family! They have to pay for that. It's time for the

Heritage Guard to take their rightful place in society and lead this nation. That's the only way our future will be secure."

Bishop's eyes lit up as he heard the enthusiasm in her voice. She pushed on, knowing she was on the right track and that her passionate words were fanning the flames of his zealousness. "I brought you Daniel as a new recruit, as well. He proved his loyalty at the bank by saving my life and getting me out of there without getting caught, even if he is law enforcement. He's a well-respected detective with the local police department, and can be very helpful to the Guard with our future projects, especially Operation Battlefield."

Bishop narrowed his eyes. "What do you know about that?"

"Not enough," she said forcefully. "Jackson only told me he needed me to get some C-4 explosives to help with the project. I'm working on that, but since he is dead, I need to know if you still want it and how much to get. He was only starting to share the plans with me before the bank job."

"Does your cop know?"

"No," she answered, her tone firm. "But he can help. Both of us can. Jackson said Operation Battlefield was going to bring more glory to the Heritage Guard than anything else we've ever done. I want to be a part of that, and I'm sure Daniel will too if you decide to bring him on board." She leaned forward. "Of course, that decision is totally up to you."

Bishop considered her plea and was silent for a few moments. Finally, he spoke. "I will consider your request, but you have to realize Daniel is untested. You've proven your loyalty by participating at the bank, but Daniel will have to show us his loyalty before he can be trusted. I'm willing to give him a chance, but he starts as a level one and has to earn his way up the ladder, just like everyone else."

Bethany was relieved by his words. "I understand, and I'm sure he will. Thank you." If Bishop was considering letting Daniel join the Guard, then even though they'd found him in the park, they wouldn't hurt him. He was probably with Guard members right now who were already sizing him up.

Bishop smiled. "I know you can get your hands on things, and we need a few items besides the C-4 for Operation Battlefield. Can you help us out?"

Bethany nodded. "Give me the list. I'll let you know what I can get and when."

"I was hoping you'd say that. Our immediate problem is funding. Since the bank robbery didn't yield any cash, we've had to come up with alternative methods to fund our operation. I'm going to put you with a new group, and your first assignment will be to help us obtain some of the money we need. After we get the money, we'll sit down and go over the Battlefield plans. Are you ready?"

Bethany nodded. "Absolutely."

"Good. Let's go meet your new family." He pushed her cell phone and gun back to her across the table and stood. She surreptitiously pushed a select number on her phone, then put it in her pocket. It only took a few short minutes to clone a phone, and then she would be able to access all of Bishop's contacts and listen in on his cell phone conversations. Things were looking up.

She said a short but heartfelt prayer of thanks. God had helped her get this mission back on track, and she was immensely grateful.

TWELVE

Bethany followed Bishop into a nearby room, and her eyes widened when she saw the scene. Daniel and Derek, a man she had only met a couple of times before, had obviously been fighting, and were being held apart by two large, bulky men who were strangers to her. Daniel's nose was bleeding again, and Derek was sporting an eye that was starting to swell and a fat lip. Furniture was strewn about and blood had been smeared on the floor and walls. It was a huge mess. Daniel's expression was angry and he pulled against the larger man's grip.

"What's going on?" she asked incredulously.

"This man is responsible for Terrell's death!" Derek cried, his eyes shooting fire. Again, he tried to free himself from a man wearing a Tampa Bay Rays hat, but the bigger man held fast.

Bethany couldn't believe what she was seeing. She'd thought that working with J.P. was difficult because he was such a hothead, but Derek was apparently just as much of a firebrand as the man they'd visited in the hospital the day before. This was her new cell?

A wave of dread swept over her. Working with this man was going to be challenging to say the least. She marched up to Derek and got right in his face. "I was at that bank. I was with Terrell. He was like a brother to me. This man had nothing to do with Terrell's death. Yes, he's a cop, but he's on our side. He saved my life, and he would have saved Terrell's too if it would have been possible."

"You're just saying that because he's your man, Hailey," Derek spat.

She moved so quickly that Derek didn't have time to react. In seconds, her automatic weapon was pressed tightly against his forehead. When she spoke, her voice was low and lethal. "Are you calling me a liar, Derek?"

The entire room got quiet and everyone was still, waiting for the scene to play out. Bethany was one of the few women in this organization, and she knew strength was valued. It was a gamble to pull her weapon when she was meeting new members of the Guard, but she wouldn't get another opportunity to make a first impression. She rolled the dice.

The man restraining Derek looked over to Bishop for guidance, and for a moment, Bethany wondered what he would do. Then she inwardly breathed a sigh of relief when she saw the older man shake his head and hold up his hand, keeping the man in the Rays baseball cap from intervening.

"Well?" She increased the pressure of the barrel of the gun on Derek's forehead.

"Fine!" he finally said under his breath.

"Fine what, Derek?" she asked, her eyes still boring into him.

"I believe you, Hailey, okay? If you say he didn't kill Terrell, then I believe you. Come on, put the gun away. Like you said. We're all on the same side."

She slowly lowered her weapon, but her eyes were narrowed. "Don't ever question my loyalty again, Derek, or Daniel's either. I trust this man with my life."

"Sure, Hailey. Whatever you say." The guy in the Rays hat released Derek and the guy wearing a flannel shirt released Daniel and handed him a bandanna that he had in his pocket. Daniel used it to staunch the blood that was running out of his nose. Daniel's poor nose! He was going to be hurting tonight. She made a mental note to buy some pain reliever for him on the way home once they got out of this meeting. He still had bruising under both of his eyes and swelling around his nose from his initial injury, and this latest knock was only going to make it worse. Just like at the bank, she had to stop herself from going to his side and fussing over his injury. This wasn't the time or place; nor would he appreciate her interference. Here, she was Hailey Weber, a tough woman who lived on the fringes, knew how to get things and fought for the Heritage Guard.

"So if we're done posturing," Bishop said, "I'd like to get down to business." He righted one of the chairs that had been knocked over during the fray, took a seat and motioned for everyone else to sit except for the man in the Rays baseball cap, who stood guard by the door. "As most of you know, my name is Bishop Jacobs.

We've suffered a major setback with the loss of Jackson and his team, but thankfully, Hailey survived and is still here to help us fight the cause. We also have some new help. You've all met Derek. As you now know, he's Terrell's cousin who just moved here from Alabama. Liam—" he nodded to the man wearing the flannel shirt "—and his brother, Ethan—" he motioned to the man wearing the Rays cap "—round out the rest of the team. We've been assigned a new project with a quick turnaround. It's going to take some planning and a lot of teamwork. We don't have time for fighting among ourselves. The timeline for Operation Battlefield has been moved up, so everything we're doing has to happen faster than we expected." He looked at Derek. "If you can't handle working with a cop, say so now and we'll find you another team."

Derek gave Daniel a look of derision but stopped when he noticed Bethany's glare. Finally, he looked back at Bishop. "If you vetted him, Bishop, that's good enough for me."

Bishop nodded. "Then the subject is closed. I don't want to hear about it again."

"So what's the job?" Liam asked, leaning forward.

Bishop pulled out some documents from a pocket inside his jacket. "We've got a friend who works inside a bank." He glanced at Bethany as if to reassure her. "Don't worry, Hailey. It's not the same one we tried to rob last week. They receive half a million dollars by armored car every month that then gets distributed to their various ATMs around town. There won't be any tracking devices or dye packs because those

don't get added until after the money gets distributed."
He leaned back and smiled. "We need that money for
Operation Battlefield. We're going to rob that armored
car when it comes to the bank to make the delivery."

"Bethany, Daniel, I'm David Hooker, your new contact at the FBI. I'll be in charge of the Heritage Guard
case going forward." Bethany had an eerie sense of déjà
vu as she shook hands with the large, middle-aged man
before taking a seat across from him at the small restaurant in Chattanooga. The mom-and-pop place was
a local favorite and was amazingly similar to the diner
they had been sitting in right before Justin Harper was
killed in the parking lot. This time though, Max Westfield was with them, sitting next to Hooker with his
laptop, taking notes as usual. Daniel also shook hands
with Hooker, then nodded at Westfield before taking
the seat next to Bethany.

Bethany surveilled the small diner, looking for
anything suspicious or out of place. Nothing seemed
overtly dangerous, so her eye strayed to a Christmas
tree that was standing in the corner that was flashing
with strands of red-and-green mini lights. Several homemade ornaments that looked like they had been made
from a homemade clay recipe of flour, salt and water
were in the size and shape of sugar cookies and decorated the tree. It was a charming piece of nostalgia that
brought back happy memories. She'd made many of the
same type of ornaments with her mom when she had
been growing up.

She pulled herself back from her recollections and

studied the new man before her. She had never seen
Special Agent Hooker before, and she was not impressed with her new handler. She couldn't put her
finger on the problem. He seemed normal enough. His
suit was dark and appeared like the normal FBI style
the agency was known for wearing, and he was fit and
clean-cut. If anything, her gut was just telling her that
David Hooker was too distracted to take her and the job
she was doing seriously. And why was Max Westfield,
a low man on the organizational ladder, even here at
this meeting? Granted, she had been away from the FBI
offices for quite a while, but something just seemed off.

"So you drew the short straw?" she asked Hooker,
partially joking, but also partly hoping that he would
contradict her and reassure her concerns.

"I wouldn't say that," Hooker said in a business tone,
"but I admit I haven't been able to get completely up
to speed on this case yet. It's only been temporarily
assigned to me during the investigation into Justin's
murder. Then the top brass will reevaluate the case in
its entirety and determine the wisest course of action
during the next few days."

Bethany's gut tightened, her fears confirmed. They
were reevaluating her case? This was the first she'd
heard of it, and she wondered if she'd even be consulted before the decision would be made to continue
the investigation or pull the plug completely. That irked
her. She needed to be a part of *any* conversation the
FBI had about the Heritage Guard case, and she should
certainly be consulted before anyone tried to shut it
down. She was about to let the agent have a piece of

her mind when she felt Daniel's hand squeeze her thigh under the table. He undoubtedly wanted to remind her to proceed cautiously. She ignored him.

"So let me get this straight. I'm putting my life on the line, and so is Detective Morley, by the way, and the FBI has given the case to someone who doesn't even have time to read the file?" She moved toward the edge of her seat as if to leave, but Hooker's no-nonsense voice stopped her.

"I'll have it read by the end of the day, Agent, and I promise you that I'll know every last detail. I take this job very seriously. I also recognize the gravity of your situation, and that of Detective Morley, I assure you."

She looked him in the eye. He seemed somber and his expression was resolute. Beside him, Westfield was smiling and his green eyes flashed, as if he had warned Hooker about her temper and had just been proven correct. She wondered if Westfield was on her side because he believed she was a good agent, or if it was only because he was interested in having a relationship with her. If she had to bet, she would guess it was the latter. Being around him still made her skin crawl. As if to accent the point, she felt Westfield's leg touch hers suggestively underneath the table. She kicked him and gave him a small smile of satisfaction when he winced.

"I'm glad to hear that," Daniel said, joining the conversation before she could dig herself any deeper into a hole she couldn't climb out of. "I'm sure Mr. Westfield has informed you that my boss, Captain Murphy, wants to be kept apprised of the details of this case since it is a joint operation between the FBI and the local authorities."

"Yes, I'm aware of that aspect of the operation," Hooker agreed. "So why don't you bring me up to speed so I can help you do your jobs."

Daniel squeezed Bethany's leg again and she gave him a look. Finally, she swallowed and gave Hooker a short overview of the Heritage Guard undercover assignment, and finished by telling him about how she had recently cloned Bishop's phone.

"I was able to download his list of contacts. If you can give me a secure site, I'll send you what I've found so far. I would imagine that many of the names from his phone are Guard members. Can you start checking them out?"

Hooker nodded. "Yes. We also need recordings of his conversations. I secured a warrant authorizing the recordings, so now they can be used in court to help our case if you hear anything useful."

"We've already worked out a way to do the recordings. Every number he dials and every word he utters is being saved. I'll start weeding through them tonight." Next, she told Hooker about their upcoming Guard assignment and every detail she knew about the armored car robbery. He was taking notes, and she was glad to see he was interested enough to do so.

"Okay, I'll get this approved and make sure there's no interference during the job. What else do you need?"

"He mentioned C-4. I don't know how much, or what else he'll want, but I imagine he'll need the detonators and timers. He said we'll talk again after the armored car heist."

Hooker raised an eyebrow. "Did he mention Operation Battlefield?"

She nodded. "Yes. I think the C-4 is going to be used for that mission. The bank job also seems like a test. If Daniel and I can help pull that off, I think he'll start trusting us with more. He seemed anxious to get the details straight. Last I heard, they had moved up the date, so whatever they're planning, they need to get their ducks in a row and fast."

Hooker wrote a few more notes, then closed his notebook. He leaned forward, his expression intense. "Okay, Agent Walker, let me tell you the bottom line. I've talked with the brass about this case. They're worried that it's been dragging out so long and they don't have anything to show for it except the fiasco at the bank. On top of that, they believe, and I agree, that Justin's murder is related. You've been given two more weeks to tie up all of the loose ends and bring this case to a close."

"Two weeks?" She pushed back from the table. "I don't think that's realistic. I can't get you what you need in that short amount of time. It's just not possible."

"Make it happen," Hooker intoned, apparently ignoring her flash of temper. "With Bishop's cell phone, you can record all sorts of conversations in the room, even if he's not using the phone. Get him to say what you need. Meanwhile, I'll be researching the list of names you send me from his contacts and cross-referencing them with what you've given us in the past from Jackson Smith's contacts. Together with Detective Morley's help, I'm confident you can get the job done."

She fumed inwardly, but it was patently obvious that he wasn't going to budge. And why should he? He wasn't the one that had devoted a year of his life to this case. All he saw was the loss of Agent Harper and the deaths at the bank, which she had to admit were very large losses. Still, if they could figure out the plans for Operation Battlefield and head off whatever the Guard was planning, they could probably still save hundreds of lives. She just didn't think two weeks was a realistic time frame.

She glanced over at Westfield. Instead of offering her support, he seemed to be trying to flirt with her with his eyes. Good grief! She wanted to shake him and kick him again. He was such a letch! Why couldn't he take the hint and keep his mind on arresting the Guards?

Daniel looked at the computer screen, still not believing his eyes. He rubbed them and leaned back. It had been a very long day, and he had been very happy to finally get back to the apartment and put his feet up. He was sitting on the couch now with his legs resting on the coffee table, sipping a soda and reading through the information that had thus far been gleaned from Bishop's phone. The FBI had some amazing software that had already made transcripts of many of the calls he had made, as well as created lists of his contacts and call records. The man had been incredibly busy since his phone had been cloned, and the information they were gleaning was a gold mine.

"Is everything okay?" Bethany asked as she came from the kitchen and sat down in the chair that was sitting kitty-corner to the couch. She had a cranberry juice bottle in her hand and she took a drink, then propped her feet up on the table next to his. He liked that she was able to relax around him and be herself. He set the laptop aside and reached for her right foot, then gently started massaging it.

"That's wonderful." She smiled. "I'll give you an hour to stop."

He laughed at her joke, but would gladly keep rubbing if it would keep her smiling. She had such a lovely smile and it lit up her entire face. "I'm impressed by the software that is capturing all of this information about Bishop. If Hooker can research the backgrounds of his contacts, we might have a pretty good membership list for the Heritage Guard."

"Yeah, Bishop seems very connected. Once we do the armored car job tomorrow, I'm hoping he'll share more of the Operation Battlefield plans with us. If he drops a few names, I'll be ready. Now that we have to come up with our case in two weeks, we'll really have to push for information. Pushing hasn't worked in the past, but maybe once I see his list of items he needs, I can think of some way to weasel the information out of him."

Daniel switched to her left foot and she sighed. When she spoke, however, her voice held a note of concern. "So are you okay with what you have to do tomorrow?

I mean, this will be the first time you've ever committed a felony. The first time I had to do it, I was sick to my stomach for hours."

Daniel was silent for a moment. He wondered how much it would change her opinion of him if she knew more about his history. He shook his head, more convinced than ever that he needed to keep his past in the past. "I'm not pleased, but I don't really have a choice. I've been praying that there isn't any collateral damage and that no innocent bystanders get hurt. Those are my main concerns."

"You're right," she agreed. "Thankfully, you're just the driver, so you won't have to pull your gun on anyone."

He put her foot down and sat back. "I keep trying to tell myself that what we're doing is for the greater good, but in my mind it's still hard to justify. Maybe once I understand the details of Operation Battlefield, my conscience will be clearer. Then it will all seem worth it. Right now, it's hard to see how it all fits together without knowing the bigger picture."

He told Bethany about how his cell phone had rung that first night they had been in the apartment, and how when he had tried to track down the phone's owner, the number had come up as untraceable. "Only you and Justin were supposed to have that number. So who could have been calling?"

"Maybe it was a wrong number?" she said hopefully.

Daniel raised an eyebrow. "Do you really believe that?"

She shook her head. "No. So if we assume the worst,

that means the Guard knows where we are staying and is probably watching our every move."

"And how did they get that information? Those phones were supposed to be clean. Justin said so himself."

He pulled the laptop over and showed her the screen he had been looking at. "We also have another problem. See this chart? It's a list of everyone Bishop has called in the last month." He pointed to three of the entries. "See these? These are to Captain Murphy, my boss."

Bethany's eyes widened and the shock was visible in her eyes. "How do you think they know each other?"

"I don't know, but we're going to have to find out. Captain Murphy grew up in this area, but I don't know anything about Bishop Jacobs. I've been searching the internet but nothing has jumped out so far. Let's hope Hooker can find some connection. It makes me wonder if Captain Murphy is the mole we've been searching for." He didn't want to believe it was true. Captain Murphy had always seemed to be an honorable man. Yes, he was rough around the edges, but he always seemed to get the job done, and he was a good cop. Could he be the reason Bethany had almost been killed at the bank? And if so, why? If he was dirty and a member of the Guard himself, why would he sanction the killing of the rest of the Guard team? Had Captain Murphy been the one who had gotten Justin killed? None of this was adding up.

Justin Harper had been right about one thing: they couldn't trust anybody.

THIRTEEN

Daniel's hands were sweaty. He wiped them on his jeans, then looked over at Bethany, who was calmly reading more of the transcripts of conversations from Bishop's phone that were saved on the laptop. Today, he would commit a crime. He hadn't broken the law since he was a teenager and he was forced to steal to survive. He hadn't realized that this undercover assignment would bring up such old memories, but between the actions he would perform this afternoon and his conversation with Bethany when he had spilled the truth about his mother, a lot of unpleasant recollections were surfacing that he thought he had buried forever.

He remembered picking the pocket of a man who had been wearing a dark green woolen jacket one cold winter evening. Daniel had bumped into the man and netted over a hundred dollars from the man's wallet. The man had also carried a picture of a young girl in the leather folds, as well as some old newspaper clippings that Daniel had never even glanced at. He'd tossed the entire thing in the trash soon after the theft, but he'd always wondered how much damage his actions had caused. Had that been the only picture of the girl the man had owned? Had his victim treasured that photo and news stories that he'd carried? Had he caused the man hours or even days of angst because of his actions?

He wondered why God was allowing all of the pain from his past to resurface, especially now when he so desperately wanted to keep it buried. What good could come from it? Yet, he did know that God would never leave him or forsake him, no matter what was happening in his life or the difficulties he faced.

Daniel glanced at Bethany again and envied her calm demeanor. She had an amazing ability to stay focused, no matter what the circumstance. It was an admirable trait, and something that no doubt made her excellent at her job. She was the consummate professional, and he had always respected her dedication and work ethic.

A wave of longing swept over him that took his breath away. He ached to just hold her in his arms. She was so beautiful. Her hair was pulled back in a ponytail, which only accented her delicate cheekbones and classic lovely features. Her eyes had always been her best feature in his mind, and were like lakes of blue on a warm summer day. It wasn't just her outer beauty that captivated him, however. Her inner strength and fortitude were just as attractive. Yet, to share himself in the way that she required would be to lay open his heart completely and would make him totally vulnerable. He didn't think he was capable of doing what she was asking. It was too hard. But could he let her go? Was it worth the sacrifice?

*Dear Lord, help me decide what to do about Beth-
any. If You want me to tell her about my past, please
give me the strength to do so. I can't do it without You.
If You don't want me to share, please help her understand. I need You. I need Your guidance. Please help
me know what to do, and lead me with Your perfect
will for my life.*

"This is it!" Bethany exclaimed, bringing him back
to the here and now. She picked up the laptop and
brought it over to the table where he was sitting and
positioned it so he could see the screen. "I've been sort-
ing through hundreds of texts and phone transcripts,
but finally found something. Bishop was talking to
someone named Bradley, and they mention Operation
Battlefield. Then they say *stadium* and *detonation.* That
can only mean one thing." Their eyes met and they said
the next words together.

"They're planning on blowing up a stadium!"

"But which one?" Daniel asked. "There are three I
can think of right off the bat. AT&T Stadium where the
Lookouts play, Engel Stadium and Finley Stadium."

Bethany opened another window on the browser
and did some quick searching. "It has to be AT&T
Stadium. They wouldn't want to do something unless
it brought maximum notoriety to their cause. According to these schedules, there's nothing planned during
the next two months at Engel or Finley. But look at
this." She pointed to the screen. "There are two events
coming up at AT&T, and look—all of the seating is
basically along the first base side, so it would take a
minimum amount of explosives to do a lot of damage."

"What are the two events?" Daniel asked, leaning closer.

"There's a marching band competition next week, and three weeks from now, there's a huge multi-state track meet." The worry was palpable in her eyes. "Good grief. It could be either one of those. Either one would be horrific."

He took her hand and squeezed it. "We need more information. Hopefully, after today's robbery they'll trust us enough to let us know more about their plans. Or if they don't, maybe Bishop will let more of the details slip."

The driver pulled the armored truck up to the bank door at exactly 3:15 p.m., right on schedule. As was the company policy, the driver stayed in his seat, surveilling the area, while the other guard got out and opened the back doors of the truck.

As soon as both of the doors were open, the robbers struck.

"Hands in the air, now!" Derek yelled. He grabbed the guard from behind, getting a good grip on the man's bulletproof vest and pulling him to the side of the truck with his left hand as he kept his gun pointed at him with his right. The guard complied and raised his hands.

"Okay, don't shoot. I'll do what you say. Please don't shoot."

Bethany appeared from the other side of the truck, her gun also pointed at the guard. All of the robbers were dressed in black pants and jackets, and they were also wearing ski masks that obscured their features. She moved to the front of the truck where the guard was standing so she had a clear view of both guards, as well as the inside of the truck. Ethan was on the other side of the armored truck, also wielding a weapon and keeping an eye on the surroundings.

"Get on your knees," she ordered.

The guard complied. His eyes were wild with fright. She was sorry for that. She didn't like this part of the job, but it was necessary. Hopefully, this would be the last crime she would be committing in the process of taking down the Heritage Guard.

"Take out your gun and put it on the concrete. Now," Derek yelled.

The guard did as he was told and Bethany kicked the gun away, just as Daniel, also dressed as the others, backed up the late model SUV to the armored truck and opened up the back. Liam jumped out of the back of the SUV and got inside the armored truck. A few seconds later, he was throwing wrapped bundles of cash into the SUV.

"Lie down on the ground," Bethany ordered, her eyes still on the guard. She looked up and saw the other guard calling in the robbery.

"The driver is calling it in," she yelled to the others. "We have fifteen seconds. Go!"

Liam threw in the last few bundles and slammed the back trunk of the SUV. "That's it. We're done. Let's go!"

Suddenly a shot rang out. Bethany looked quickly at both of the guards, but neither one of them had fired the shot. Her eyes flew over to Derek, who was loosely holding a pistol in his hand that he had taken off one of the guards, then toward Daniel, who was still sitting in the driver's seat of the vehicle. The bullet had hit the frame of the SUV only inches from his head.

Daniel, wearing his mask, got out of the van and slammed the door, his eyes blazing. His weapon was pointed at Derek's head. "If you're going to try to kill me, you'd better not miss the next time!"

"The gun just went off. I wasn't aiming for you," Derek said, holding the pistol up, the barrel pointing to the sky. They couldn't see his face beneath the mask, but his voice held a smirk. Bethany felt a surge of relief that Daniel hadn't been hurt and took a step toward Derek, ready for some retribution, but Liam reached him first and grabbed his collar.

"You idiot! You'd jeopardize our plans here and now? For what?"

Derek tried to pull away, but Liam grabbed the pistol away from him, secured it in his own waistband, and pushed him to the ground. "Keep your eye on the ball."

"Don't you care about Terrell?" Derek yelled.

A siren sounded in the distance and Bethany motioned with her gun. "We've got to move. We'll hash this out later."

Bethany met Daniel's eyes and nodded. They both understood that they had to do something about Derek, but it had to be done later when the police weren't breathing down their necks. Derek was a hothead who wasn't going to roll over no matter what the Heritage Guard ordered him to do, and it was obvious that Daniel was in danger as long as Derek was in the picture. He could ruin all of their plans if something wasn't done to control him.

Daniel got back behind the wheel and Bethany joined him in the front seat. Liam got in the back, and a few seconds later, Derek and Ethan joined them and slammed the door closed. As soon as the door was closed, Daniel hit the gas and the SUV sped away. The entire robbery, including the stray shot, had been completed in under four minutes.

"Woo-hoo!" Derek yelled, when they were about five miles away and still not being followed. "We did it!" He drummed on the seat in front of him with his hands as if he was still trying to burn off some excess energy.

No one answered him and the entire group pulled their masks off and began to let the adrenaline that had come from the robbery slowly escape. Everyone except Daniel, that is. Bethany could tell that Daniel was still burning about the bullet that had hit only inches from his head. His lips were pulled into a thin line and his eyes were narrowed as he drove, focused on the road before him.

After a few turns, Daniel pulled the SUV into the parking lot of the car rental company, which was the prearranged site where they would all separate. Bishop was waiting and came out of the office and met the car when they arrived. He approached Ethan, who was the official leader of the group, but before a word could be said Daniel had pulled Derek out of the car, pushed him up against the side of the SUV and punched him hard in the face. Blood oozed from the wound as Daniel hit him a second time before Liam and Ethan were able to pull him off and separate the two. Derek swiped at the blood and then pulled his fist back as if he was going to hit Daniel, now that he was secured, but Bethany stepped between them.

"No way, Derek. You deserved that, and more."

"What's going on?" Bishop demanded. "Did you have trouble on the job?"

"The job went just fine," Liam answered, "until Derek took a shot at Daniel's head."

"It was a stray bullet," Derek whined as he wiped at the blood from his lip. "I wasn't aiming for him. The gun just went off."

Daniel pulled against Liam and Ethan's grip. "Liar. You were trying to kill me."

Bishop raised an eyebrow. "Ethan?" He looked to the leader, apparently wanting some clear direction from the one who had run the job and could give him an unbiased opinion.

Ethan met his eye. "We got the money and it's in the back. Derek was either very sloppy or intentionally took a shot at Daniel. Either way, I don't want him on my team again. He can't be trusted."

Derek suddenly turned all of his anger on Ethan. His face was flushed with rage and even more blood bubbled out of his nose. "What? How can you take his side? He's a cop, just like those cops who killed Terrell! He's the enemy."

"I'm not taking sides. I'm trying to do what's best for the Heritage Guard. That's the reason why we're out here doing what we're doing in the first place," Ethan said in a matter-of-fact tone. "When you make it personal, you make mistakes and people get hurt. That's not how I operate."

Bishop put his hands up in a motion of surrender. "Ethan is right. I'm sorry, Derek, but we can't use you anymore. You're out."

Derek looked like he was going to explode. "What?"

"You heard me," Bishop repeated. "Clear out of here."

Derek's face turned even redder, and he looked around as if he was trying to find something to throw or kick. Seeing nothing, he charged toward Daniel, but Ethan released Daniel, crossed his arms and blocked Derek with a move that looked like it came from a football field. Derek ended up on the ground with gravel embedded into his hands and face, and he brushed it away angrily. He apparently realized that physically he wasn't going to get anywhere today, so the venom spewed from his mouth instead.

"You'll be sorry," he spat. "You'll fail without me. Just wait and see."

"I'd advise you to go quietly," Bishop said, his voice calm in the middle of a storm. "You don't need to make enemies of the Guard."

Derek fisted his palms and looked from one face to another. He finally knelt over and picked up his wool mask that he had lost during the scuffle, then turned and started walking away from the group, a scowl still on his face.

Once he had disappeared, Daniel turned back to

Bishop and handed him the keys to the SUV. "The money is in the back. Unfortunately, there's also a bullet hole that will need to be repaired."

Bishop took the keys and pocketed them. "Congratulations on a job well done."

Daniel pulled Bethany against him and kissed her cheek. "Success, darling." Still holding her, he turned toward Ethan. "What's next?"

"Disappear," Ethan said, an enigmatic smile on his face. "We'll contact you shortly for the next job."

Bishop pointed to Bethany. "I need to speak to you. Without your boyfriend."

Bethany shrugged and kissed Daniel on the lips, then pulled away from him. "I'll catch up with you later."

Daniel watched her follow Bishop into the small building. His lips burned from her kiss. He knew it had been for show, but he still enjoyed it. He wanted to follow after her into the meeting to make sure she was safe, but it was obvious that he wasn't invited; he knew she could take care of herself and that the danger was minimal. He needed to do some research anyway on the stadium, and this was the perfect opportunity to do so. He pulled his keys out of his pocket and headed to his truck, saying a prayer for her safety as he did so, just in case.

Bethany took the chair that was offered to her and leaned back, keeping her back to the wall so she could see everyone in the small room, as well as the door. The room was furnished with only a small desk, a floor lamp and a few chairs. A car rental poster was plastered on the wall, advertising the latest specials. She glanced around the room and felt a measure of relief. She knew Bishop and also the large man standing by the door, but it paid to be cautious, so she kept a wary eye open, just in case she needed to act quickly. Her pistol was in her waistband, and she had another spare sidearm tucked in her boot, as an extra precaution.

Bishop took the seat across from her. "Good job today. Any problems?"

She shook her head. "Only that issue with Derek. The rest went off like clockwork. We emptied out the truck and no one was hurt, and all within the time frame allotted. It was a clean job."

"I'm glad to hear it. The money will be put to good use." He leaned forward. "We need fifteen to twenty blocks of C-4, as well as the ribbon charges to set them off, and timers for each of the blocks. Can you help us?"

She whistled between her teeth. "Wow. That's a big order. When do you need it?"

"Four days."

She leaned back. "You don't ask much."

"We've got the money to pay—now that today's job was successful."

"You'll have to pay a bit more than the going rate if you want it that quickly."

Bishop smiled, but there was a malevolent air to his attitude. "Make the deal. I'll get you the money."

"Will do," she said with a nod. "You have someone who knows how to set it up?"

"Don't you worry about that. You just get the explosives. We'll take care of the rest." He took his cap off and ran his hands through his hair.

"Do you need anything else?"

Bishop shook his head. "We'll let you know."

The tone of his voice said the meeting was over, so she stood, nodded to each of the men and left the room. She'd ridden with Daniel to the meeting site for the armored car heist, so now she started walking away from the car rental company toward the downtown area. She pulled out her cell phone and couldn't reach Hooker, even after several attempts, so she tried Westfield next. He answered on the first ring.

"Bethany. It's good to hear from you. Is everything okay?"

"Max, I can't get Hooker. Any idea why he's not answering?"

"I'm not sure, but I can tell you this. They've decided to pull you in and close the investigation."

Indignation rose in her throat. "They can't do that! He gave me two weeks!"

"Have you made any progress?" Westfield asked.

"Yes, we think we've identified their target, and they want me to buy the C-4 for them. Everything is coming to a head. We'll lose this opportunity if we pull out now. I really need you to talk to Hooker and change his mind. Can you do that?"

"I can try, but it won't be easy."

A wave of alarm spread over her. She couldn't let this investigation fail now. She had invested too much, and she needed Westfield on her side. "Please, Max, do what you can. I also need fifteen to twenty blocks of C-4 in four days, along with the ribbon charges and timers. This is the one, Max. It all comes down to this." In the past, Justin had always gotten her what she needed to maintain her cover. If Hooker couldn't help, she desperately needed Westfield to come through. If the Guard wanted the C-4 in four days and they were planning on blowing up AT&T Stadium, then the upcoming marching band competition was the likely target, and she had to do everything in her power to stop them before it was too late.

"Can you get me the C-4, Max?"

"I don't know, Bethany. That's a pretty tall order, especially with the brass wanting to shut down the investigation. Like I said, it won't be easy."

"It's the last thing I need. The Guard has been putting all of their efforts into Operation Battlefield. This C-4 has got to be for that mission. If I can provide the explosives, they'll include me in the planning, and I can learn all of the details. Once I know what's going on, we'll be able to stop them."

"We seized some C-4 from a case about three years ago that is still in the evidence locker. I may be able to get you a few blocks off the record, but I don't know about twenty."

"Off the record? What does that mean exactly? I don't want you to do anything that will jeopardize this case." His comment surprised her. Even though the brass were in a hurry to have this case concluded, there were still procedures in place that had to be followed when it came to using FBI supplies for a job—

especially for munitions. Was Westfield going to steal the explosives?

"Nothing. That's not what I meant. Of course, I'll go through official channels. I'm just under a lot of pressure to finish this case, just like you are, Bethany. Can't you do it with less?"

His tone was filled with exasperation, so she pushed on, filing her concerns in the back of her mind to consider later. "I've got to have at least fifteen."

She heard Westfield sigh. "You're asking a lot from me, Bethany."

"Max, this is the culmination of my entire undercover operation. The arrests will be significant. I'll share the credit with you. I'll make sure everyone knows that you're the one that made the operation possible. If we're successful, it will mean a big boost for your career."

She heard him sigh again. "Bethany, I want to be promoted, sure, but I have feelings for you. Strong feelings. I must have been very clumsy with telling you about how I feel, but I'm telling you know. I think I'm in love with you."

Good grief! This is not what she had expected when she'd dialed Westfield's line. She didn't share his feelings, but she needed his help and didn't know how to get it and let him down gently at the same time. She opted for the truth, since she wasn't good at subterfuge when it came to relationships. "Look, Max, I appreciate you telling me how you feel, so I'll be honest with you right back. Daniel and I used to have a very committed relationship, and lately since we've been working together again, we've talked about getting back together. I don't know where it's all going to lead, but I'm really not ready to date anyone else until I know for sure if that relationship is going to go somewhere or not." She didn't know how to even describe her relationship with Daniel right now, but she did know that she didn't want to pursue anything with Westfield, regardless of what happened with Daniel. She didn't want to hurt him though, so this was her way of trying to let him down as easily as possible. She paused, but when he didn't comment, she continued, hoping that he understood. "Does that make any sense at all?"

"I guess," he admitted, finally breaking the silence. "I can't say I'm not disappointed. But I'll respect your decision. I'll check into the C-4 and let you know what I can do."

"Thanks, Max." She hung up, and stored her phone, still ruminating on what she had learned during the call.

Westfield's words seemed appropriate, but there was something in his voice that seemed sinister and sent a chill down her spine. She had always felt a bit strange around him, but he had never seemed dangerous to her until today. Could she trust Westfield? Someone had murdered Justin. She had no proof that his murder was directly related to her investigation, but she couldn't prove it wasn't related either.

She thought back through their conversation. Westfield had basically offered to steal C-4 from the evidence locker to help her, even though he backpedaled when she questioned him. Had it been just a slip of the

tongue? She knew for a fact that Justin had always req-
uisitioned what she needed to bolster her undercover
operation. Her former boss had always followed the
rules and left a paper trail a mile wide. Would Westfield actually steal the C-4 from the evidence room?
He claimed her bosses were trying to shut her operation down immediately, but she hadn't heard that from
Hooker, and even if it were true, Westfield should never
have volunteered to steal the C-4. It was a crime.

Thoughts that she had never considered began to
swarm in her mind. Was this the first time Westfield
had considered stealing evidence, or had he done it
before? Had he stolen C-4 in the past and used it to
kill Justin?

But what possible motive could he have? Justin had
hand-picked Westfield to be his assistant, and the two
men had seemed to have a good working relationship.
But if not Westfield, then who? Who else would want
to take Justin's life?

There were too many questions. Westfield might be
a bit creepy, but as far as she knew, he was a top-notch
FBI agent who had an excellent reputation. Surely his
comment today had just been a mistake. As Westfield
himself had said, they were all under a lot of pressure
to bring this case to a swift and successful conclusion.
People under stress misspoke. It happened.

Bethany sighed and rubbed the muscles in her neck.
Even she was feeling a bit edgy. For the first time in a
very long time, she found herself glad that she could
share her burden with Daniel and bounce ideas off

him. She found herself looking forward to seeing him tonight. She quickened her step toward the bus stop to grab a ride back to the apartment they were sharing. It was going to be a long night.

FOURTEEN

Bishop looked in the duffel bag that Bethany offered, then zipped it up and met her eye, disappointment heavy in his features. "Eight bricks? That's it?"

"It's a start, Bishop. I'm working on the rest." Bethany had met with Westfield early in the morning and gotten the eight bricks of C-4 from him, but it had been an awkward exchange. They had barely spoken during the few minutes it had taken to hand off the explosives. She still had not heard from Hooker, even though she had tried several times to contact him, and through several means. All she could guess was that her superiors had decided that her investigation was winding down or was canceled outright and had left Westfield in charge to tie up the loose ends. It was odd, but she had been left out of the loop for so long that she didn't know what else to think. After Justin's dire warning about the mole, she didn't know who she could trust at the FBI and dared not try to contact anyone else at the bureau—at least not until this case was well and truly over.

"You know this is time-sensitive, right?" Liam growled.

"Of course, I do," Bethany said defensively. "But C-4 isn't something you can buy at Walmart, and I wasn't given a large time frame in which to operate. I'm doing the best I can."

Liam made a derisory sound. "Maybe your boyfriend can do better. Let's bring him in here and find out. Maybe he has better connections than you do."

Bethany's stomach constricted. If they brought Daniel in, what would he say? She and Daniel were already working on getting the extra C-4 they needed from Daniel's boss, Captain Murphy, and the local Chattanooga Police Force, but so far they hadn't been able to get the delivery confirmed. They also had hoped that dealing with Captain Murphy would help them determine if he was the mole or not. However, they hadn't learned anything new. One thing they did realize—if Murphy couldn't get them the explosives they needed, they would have to start looking at alternatives, and fast. Either way, they hadn't planned on having this conversation in front of Liam, and she didn't know how Daniel would answer the interrogation.

Could she trust Daniel to say the right thing? As Daniel entered the room, their eyes met, and she wondered if he could see the fear mirrored in her own. This situation exemplified why she worked alone. When she worked undercover by herself, she didn't have to worry about anybody making a mistake and putting her life at risk. She didn't have to depend on anyone else but herself. It was lonely, but it was easier.

With Daniel, however, there was even more to it. With her boyfriend before Daniel, the man had cheated on her and then humiliated her in front of her friends. He had said terrible things that had made it hard for her to ever trust a man again on a personal level. Would Daniel humiliate her now? A year ago, when Daniel had gotten too close and started talking about marriage, it had been easier to push him away than it had been to trust him not to hurt her like her ex had done, especially since he wasn't willing to share his past with her. She preferred the loneliness to the pain. It was safer. Over the past few days, Daniel had slowly started breaking down her defenses again, and it scared her, both professionally and personally.

What would he do now? This was his first time undercover. Would he make a rookie mistake? Would he throw her under the bus to look good and score points with the Guard? Would he humiliate her for the sake of his male pride? Anything was possible, and she braced herself, not sure what to expect.

"Daniel, Hailey here says she's having some trouble getting the C-4 we need for our Operation Battlefield," Bishop said in a matter-of-fact tone. "Can you do any better?"

Daniel raised an eyebrow and Bethany's stomach clenched again, waiting for his response. He looked from Bishop to Liam, then at Bethany. "Has Hailey ever let you down in the past?"

Bishop thought about that for moment, then responded, "No. She's always proven herself to be very responsible." Even Liam shook his head once he considered Daniel's point.

Daniel shrugged. "Then I'd quit worrying. I'm not

going to be able to do any better than she can. She's the expert. You've trusted her in the past. I'd trust her now."

Bethany let out the breath she hadn't even known she was holding. Daniel had said the perfect thing, and diffused the situation with just a few simple words. She silently mouthed the words *thank you* to him and he winked in response, then turned and left the room.

"Somebody is following us," Daniel said quietly. He tried to keep the frustration out of his voice as he glanced at his rearview mirror, but he wasn't successful.

Bethany looked behind them, then quickly faced forward again. "The black sedan?"

"Yeah. I've changed lanes twice and he's staying with me."

"Can you tell who's driving?"

"A white male wearing a black watchman's cap and sunglasses. That's about all I can tell. He picked us up about ten minutes ago."

"Good grief. That could be anyone." Her voice held her own note of frustration.

Daniel didn't blame her. Another day had passed and they had still not been able to talk to Hooker, despite trying a new number that Westfield had provided. They had been able to contact Captain Murphy about the C-4, and he had agreed to provide them with the additional seven bricks they needed, so they were on their way to meet him. So far he hadn't let anything slip that made him seem like the mole, but they were both on high alert while dealing with the man, just in case.

The captain had only one condition during their conversations to get the explosives—that the Chattanooga Police Department would share in the arrests at the stadium and in the credit for the joint operation's success once the indictments were handed down. Since that had always been part of the original agreement of this joint operation, it was easy to agree. But Captain Murphy wanted to be absolutely sure that CPD wouldn't be left on the sidelines, so Daniel had done his best to reassure him that CPD would be included.

Daniel and Bethany still had their doubts about Captain Murphy and his history with Bishop Jacobs, but to date they couldn't prove anything beyond the fact that they knew each other and had talked to each other on the phone. Bishop Jacobs owned a rental car company, and as far as they knew, the captain had rented a car from him—nothing more. Still, they both harbored suspicions of the man, and had agreed to be extra careful during the exchange. They needed the FBI's help to run background checks on their suspects and right now, they just weren't getting the help they needed to find the connections to build their case, or prove Murphy's guilt or innocence.

Daniel looked into the rearview mirror again and changed lanes, then grimaced as he watched the car tailing them do the same once again. He glanced over at Bethany and could tell that she was getting restless and nervous.

He thought through everything that had happened

during the short time since he had gotten Bethany back in his life. Her entire Guard team were killed at the bank, someone killed her boss at the FBI and Derek tried to kill Daniel at the armored car robbery. Related or not, there were a lot of people dying all around them, and it felt like they were no closer to figuring out how everything was connected than they were when they'd started. And now, someone was following them. Was it someone from the FBI? Someone from the Guard? Or was Derek trying to get his revenge for Terrell's death?

He reached across and squeezed her hand, then released her and put both hands on the wheel. "Hold on." With a quick turn and squealing tires, he cut the truck in front of another vehicle and executed a U-turn, then maneuvered the truck into a large alley behind a warehouse that fronted an entire city block. Gravel spit from beneath his tires and water and debris spewed as he raced along, dodging obstacles along the way. He could hear car horns and traffic squawking in the wake of his driving, but he ignored it all as he sped to the end of the alley and made a quick left, then entered the street and flow of traffic. He changed lanes several more times, speeding around three more cars before he was finally stopped at a red light.

"Any sign of them?"

Bethany didn't answer and he glanced in her direction. She was as white as a sheet and had pressed herself as close as possible to the truck door. She was also clinging for dear life to the seat belt and the grab handle on the ceiling. Her knuckles had turned white where she gripped the plastic for all it was worth.

He laughed. He couldn't help himself. The look on her face was just too comical to ignore. "Are you okay?"

She shook her head. "No. You're crazy!" The tone of her voice made it perfectly clear what she thought of his driving.

"What?" he raised an eyebrow, giving her his best innocent look. He'd totally forgotten that she got motion sickness if he drove too fast and made too many quick turns in the vehicle. Bethany was tough as nails 99 percent of the time. It was almost refreshing to be reminded that she was human after all and had weaknesses like the rest of the people on the planet.

"Remind me to never let you drive anywhere ever again," she said under her breath. "I think I'm going to throw up all over your nice floor mats."

"Come on. I'm a good driver," he said with a smile.

She narrowed her eyes. "At least tell me you lost our tail."

"Yep."

"Then it was worth it." She moaned. "I guess," she qualified.

He drove in relative silence for another fifteen minutes or so until they arrived at a small brick building that was near the outskirts of town. Pine trees and rocky outcrops surrounded the area, and the other nearby buildings seemed to be abandoned, with no signs of life. It was about ten in the morning, so there was plenty of sunlight to help them see their surroundings, but it was strange that no other cars or people were anywhere nearby.

Daniel pulled up behind the storefront and killed the engine, then turned to Bethany. "Okay. Are you ready for this?"

Bethany shrugged. "Ready as I'll ever be. I'm feeling better now." They got out of their truck and closed the doors, looking warily around them. "Are you sure you have the right address? This is a strange meeting place."

"Yes, I double-checked it," Daniel answered. He glanced at his watch. "We're right on time. Captain Murphy said he'd meet us here, and he's usually a very punctual man. Let's give him a couple of minutes. Maybe he's just running late."

He noticed that Bethany still seemed a bit unsteady. "Are you sure you're feeling alright?" When she didn't answer, he reached over and took Bethany's hand, then pulled her closer as they locked eyes. His look was searching, asking for permission to go further. When he saw no resistance, he pulled her into an embrace.

"I'm really sorry my driving made you sick." He gently took his thumb and ran it slowly down the side of her cheek. Her skin was soft like rose petals. "You're so beautiful." He moved his thumb and drew it across her bottom lip, then gently cupped her head with his hands and drew her even closer as his lips met hers. Electricity seemed to sizzle between them and his heart was beating like a bass drum so loudly it felt like it was coming out of his chest.

"I guess I forgive you," she murmured against him. She pulled back a bit and he could see a smile as it slowly crossed her face, yet there was hesitance in her eyes. Still, she had responded to his overtures even though nobody was around, so she was clearly not acting a role. The thought pleased him immensely.

Suddenly, they heard a car approach and the intimate mood instantly dissipated. They broke apart and she took a few steps back. She turned away from him, her eyes wide, and she covered her mouth with the back of her hand. She looked as if she was trying to compose herself as the car pulled up beside the truck and parked.

Daniel recovered first and met Captain Murphy as he got out of the car. He hoped to draw attention away from Bethany and any embarrassment she might be feeling. The police chief stood and nodded his hello, swinging a set of keys in his hand.

"Good to see you, son. I'm glad we were able to come to an understanding here. You're doing excellent work with the FBI."

"It is a joint operation, Captain. There's no reason why CPD and the FBI can't both get credit for any arrests that come from this undercover assignment. Our mutual goal is to stop the Guard before anyone else gets hurt."

Captain Murphy turned and went to the trunk of his car, opened it and pulled out a dark green duffel bag. He handed the bag to Bethany. She took it and unzipped it, then showed the contents to Daniel. He saw the bricks of C-4 inside, as well as the detonators.

"How many are in there?" he asked.

"Seven bricks, just like you asked," Captain Murphy answered.

Bethany zipped it closed and slung the bag on her back. "This has been a huge help for our mission," she said. "Thank you. You really came through for us." Despite her words, she narrowed her eyes and rested her free hand on the butt of her pistol. "Even so, we have some questions to ask you about your relationship with Bishop Jacobs."

Captain Murphy raised an eyebrow. "What do you want to know?"

Daniel stepped forward. "He is a member of the Heritage Guard. And we know you've had contact with him on several occasions lately. Can you explain that?"

Murphy straightened as his muscles tightened, but a moment later he relaxed again. "We were fraternity brothers back in college. I didn't really hang out with his crowd all that much, but we're having a reunion of sorts in a month or so and I was contacting all of the guys to invite them to the festivities. Somehow, I drew the short straw and had to make all of the phone calls." He paused, his face thoughtful. "Bishop was a little odd, but I can't see him as a terrorist. Are you sure he is part of the Guard?"

Before either of them had an opportunity to answer Murphy, a shot rang out, clipping a tree only a few feet behind them. They all heard the bullet whiz by their heads and instantly dropped to the ground, searching for cover. More bullets followed, several ricocheting off the rocks on the road and the boulders that were sporadically strewn around the landscaping. Other bullets hit the building, the vehicles or imbedded into the wood of the trees behind them. They crouched down behind the truck Bethany and Daniel had arrived in, using it for cover as they kept it between them and the gunman.

"Only one shooter?" Bethany asked as she turned and fired her 9 mm in the direction of the sniper.

"It appears so," Daniel answered as he checked his ammunition supply in his own sidearm. The bullets all seemed to be coming from the same direction and location, but since none of them had a rifle with them, they couldn't stop the sniper from firing at them. None of their handguns had anywhere near the range or accuracy of a rifle. The best they could do was lay down some cover fire while they tried to escape. The truck had taken some shots, but still seemed drivable. Since Captain Murphy had parked between the shooter and the truck, his vehicle had taken the brunt of the rounds.

"Were you followed?" Daniel asked as he snapped his clip back into his firearm.

"I didn't see anyone, but I guess anything is possible," the captain answered. "I wasn't expecting trouble. Were you?"

"Not like this," Daniel replied, sending even more rounds toward their aggressor.

"Let's get out of here," Bethany said as she threw the bag with the C-4 in the back of the truck. "Cover me," she said, meeting Daniel's eye.

She fired two more shots, then opened the passenger door and slid in, staying down and out of sight as she did so. Daniel fired at the sniper to keep him occupied, then followed her through the passenger door and into the truck as Captain Murphy fired at the shooter. He crawled over her to the driver's seat, then started the engine and rolled down the window so he could fire while Captain Murphy got into the truck. They all stayed as low as possible while Daniel backed up, spun the truck around and sped away from the building. Bullets followed them, and even though one hit the top metal door frame behind them and a few hit the side of the truck, they ended up escaping unharmed.

Daniel didn't know what to think. Was Murphy innocent? After all, he had almost been killed during the C-4 exchange. Or had that entire scene just been a clever ruse to make it look like his life was in danger to throw them off the trail? Had he and Bishop really been fraternity brothers? It was easy enough to prove or disprove with a small amount of research. Was Murphy a Guard member or not? Daniel was more unsure now than ever. After all, his phone clearly showed that Murphy had ties with Guard members who were knee-deep in suspicious activities. Were those ties innocent, as Murphy claimed? Or was he the one who had killed Justin?

Lord, please help me sort through all of the lies and get down to the truth. And thank You for protecting us today. Please help us stay safe, and figure this case out so the Heritage Guard is stopped completely before anyone else gets hurt.

FIFTEEN

Hooker shook his head, his hands on his hips. "I don't understand why you haven't been contacting me, Agent Walker. I also don't understand why I had to be contacted by Captain Murphy of the local police force to set up this meeting today. Captain Murphy reported to me that my agent was shot at and nearly killed by a sniper. That's information I should have been told by my agent, don't you think?"

Bethany raised her eyebrows, but to her credit, she held her tongue and gathered her thoughts before responding, even though Daniel could tell she was livid by his lack of insight. Daniel was also surprised by his questions. They had both followed FBI protocol to the letter, but they had been unable to get any response from Special Agent Hooker ever since he had taken over the investigation. Was the man totally out of the loop, or just incompetent?

"Sir, I've been calling you constantly without getting a reply," Bethany answered, her voice professional and controlled. "I've been leaving messages for you on a regular basis, and have sent texts and emails. In fact, Max Westfield told me that you were shutting down the operation, so I even doubled my efforts to get in touch with you. I *wanted* to communicate with you to convince you not to give up on this investigation. I still think it's worth the time and effort to keep pushing ahead, sir."

"Well, there's obviously been a communication breakdown here, Agent. Mr. Westfield claims you demanded that he provide you with fifteen blocks of C-4, and when he couldn't get the amount of explosives you demanded, you broke off communication with him and went rogue. For my part, I haven't heard from you since I was first introduced to you when I took over the case, and I'd like to know why. All I know about you is that you are involved in a highly dangerous mission, and we've already lost one agent for reasons unknown. I don't want to lose another."

Bethany was obviously struck speechless. If Westfield had been there in the small room, she probably would have gone ballistic on him, but since only the three of them were at this meeting, all she could do was start pacing to get the anger and frustration out of her system. Daniel barely knew Max Westfield, but the pieces just didn't seem to fit together. Why was he torpedoing the mission? What was his game? Daniel didn't like the guy because of the way he flirted with Bethany, but until now, he hadn't understood the depths of his treachery. He watched Bethany carefully, knowing she was close to the boiling point. Her face was flushed and her jaw had tightened. He stepped forward, diverting Hooker's attention and giving Bethany a chance to cool down.

"Mr. Westfield is giving you bad information, sir," he said quietly. "We have both tried to contact you on several occasions, especially after the armored car heist. Here are the numbers we were given to reach you." He pulled out his cell phone and read off the numbers. "The first two seem to have been disconnected. The third allowed us to leave messages, which we did, with no response. We can also provide you with texts and emails. Both Agent Walker and I left several for you, sir. We got no response."

Hooker took down the numbers and shook his head again. "Well, I don't have an explanation. Those are not my numbers. I don't even recognize those as FBI numbers. Where did you get them?"

Daniel stowed his phone. "Justin gave us each cell phones that were supposed be clean right before his death. Everything else was provided by Mr. Westfield."

"As long as we're putting our cards on the table, have you been able to discover who killed Justin?" Bethany asked.

Daniel was pleased that she had calmed down and was engaged again in the conversation.

Hooker shook his head. "We've discovered where the explosives came from and how they were detonated, but we haven't been able to tie them to any group or individual yet."

"Where did the explosives come from?" Bethany asked.

"They were stolen from the evidence locker. They

were actually logged in as evidence on one of Justin's old cases."

Bethany raised an eyebrow. "Westfield told me he was going to steal the C-4 I requested from the evidence locker too. When I called him on it, he said it was just a slip of the tongue and he was actually going through official channels, but now I'm thinking he really meant it. If you check how much is missing, I'll bet it lines up with what he gave me, and what was used to kill Justin." She leaned forward. "Do you know for sure if his death was related to my case, or one of his other cases?" she asked.

Hooker shrugged. "We honestly don't know, Agent Walker. It's still too early in the investigation to know for sure, but you've given me some good information to research when I get back to the office."

Daniel's and Bethany's eyes met. He asked her the silent question, and she agreed by nodding her head. He turned to Agent Hooker. "You should know that Justin told us there was a mole in law enforcement, sir, right before he was killed. He didn't know who, but he was just starting to investigate it before his death. He thought the mole was somehow connected with the Heritage Guard and Bethany's case. From what we know now, it looks like Westfield is that mole."

Hooker raked his hand through his hair and grimaced. He leaned forward, his body rigid with anger. "You're telling me this now?"

"We didn't know if you were the mole or not," Bethany said, her tone matter-of-fact.

Hooker turned and looked her in the eye. "I'm going

to forget you said that, Agent." His voice was low and fuming.

"Someone tried to kill us yesterday when we got the extra C-4 from Captain Murphy," Daniel said, pointedly. "A sniper was taking shots at us and we barely escaped. Bethany was also almost killed during the bank robbery, and Justin was killed right after talking to us. It might have been wrong of us to withhold that information, but you have to realize that right now, we're just not sure whom we can trust. When we couldn't get hold of you, well, we didn't know who else to contact within the FBI that we could trust either. Agent Walker has been out in the field for almost a year with Justin and Westfield as her only contacts. We're taking a big leap of faith by even talking to you now."

A moment passed, then another. The room was silent as the FBI boss pondered the situation, his eyes boring into Bethany. "Then I need to bring you in," Hooker finally replied, taking his eyes from the younger agent's. "If you're in that much danger, I can't continue putting your lives at risk."

"No!" Bethany said, her stance adamant. "We're too close. We've been called in this afternoon to help plan Operation Battlefield. This is the culmination of what we've been working for during this entire mission. If we stop now, then all of the risk, even Justin's death, will have been for nothing."

Hooker pondered the situation a few moments more, then pulled out a chair and motioned for them to sit, as well. "I admire your passion, but are you sure it's worth the risk? At this point, Westfield has to suspect that we're on to him. For all we know, he's already blown your cover with the Guard and you've both got targets on your backs."

Bethany and Daniel looked at each other, then answered together.

"Yes. It's worth it."

"In fact," Bethany added, "if Westfield did suspect anything, we'd be dead already. Our covers must still be intact."

Hooker let a few more minutes pass as he processed all of the information. Finally, he ran his hand through his hair again and sighed. "Okay. Tell me where we are. And don't leave out a single detail. I'll be contacting the attorney general's office later today to make sure they are up to date, as well. I want them ready to issue indictments as soon as we start making arrests."

Daniel was relieved. Maybe this man was going to be an ally after all. The three sat, then brought Hooker up to speed on the entire investigation. The situation was coming to a head quickly and they needed him on their side. Daniel just hoped their trust wasn't misplaced.

Bethany stood, the anger seething inside of her. For the second time today, she was boiling with anger. "Him? You invited him to this meeting?"

Derek swaggered in and pulled up a chair next to Bethany, his smile more of a smirk. He winked at her and wiggled his shoulders cheekily. "Turns out I'm valuable to the Guard after all."

Bishop held up his hands, palms out, almost as if he

were apologizing. "Some things are out of my control. I advise you to accept it and move on."

"You should be happy." Derek smirked, ignoring Bishop's comments. "They let your boyfriend come too."

Bethany glanced behind her and caught Daniel's eye. This was bad. But Derek had a point—it was a bit odd that Daniel had been invited to the meeting. But he had just proven himself at the armored car heist, so his presence wasn't altogether out of the ordinary. Derek's situation was a different story. Derek had clearly been thrown out of the Guard. There were only a handful of reasons they would have allowed him to come back, and none of them were good. Were they going to use him as a fall guy? Or had he found out Bethany or Daniel's true identity and traded that information for a seat at the table? Anxiety burned through her stomach. Derek was staring at her and smiling in a leering way that made her skin crawl. Was he a leech, or did he know she was FBI? Was she blown? She couldn't think of a single good reason why he had been invited back into the fold, and the situation was extra dangerous now that Westfield's treachery had been discovered.

Daniel gave an infinitesimal shrug and she looked away. It was too late now to turn back. She was all in. This was the meeting to plan Operation Battlefield— the one she had been waiting for. When the call had come, she'd answered it with her eyes wide open, ready for the culmination of her last year's work to finally come to fruition.

Bishop pulled out some blueprints and unrolled

them on the large table that they circled. "As some of you might have guessed, we're going to bomb AT&T Stadium this coming weekend. Hailey has brought us the C-4, detonators and timers. She'll be working with Derek, Daniel, Liam and Ethan. After they set all the charges, we'll have them rigged with timers so they'll blow at about 1:00 p.m." He pointed to several places on the blueprints. "We want the charges placed here... here...and here." He pointed to another section. "And here along this structural beam." He pulled out some brochures. "There's a high school band competition going on there this weekend, so unfortunately there will be some collateral damage."

Bethany's eyes widened. "Sounds like there will be quite a lot of lives lost if we blow it in the afternoon. Shouldn't we aim for a different time when we won't hurt so many innocent people?"

Bishop gave her a cold stare as if she was a heretic, and Bethany instantly knew that she had said the wrong thing. "If you're not with us, you're against us," he growled.

Bethany narrowed her eyes. A strong offense was always a good defense in her book. "I'm with you, Bishop. You know that. I just don't like hurting innocent children."

Bishop studied her for a moment, as if weighing her answer, then nodded. "I understand, but every decision we make has a reason. Those who made this plan determined that the sacrifice was necessary for the greater good. I know you have a soft heart. I heard what you did for J.P. at that bank job. But all I can tell you is that this is phase one of the project. All of the pieces have to fit together like a jigsaw puzzle, or no one will be able to see the bigger picture come together."

"Well, what is the greater good? If this is phase one, what is phase two? I've proven my loyalty to the Guard, and I'd like to know the big picture. Can't you tell us why we're doing this?"

Bishop tilted his head. "No, I'm sorry. I can't."

She weighed his answer. It wouldn't do any good to keep pushing, and it might even cause more problems. She decided a strategic retreat was in order. "Alright, Bishop. I trust you, and I trust the leadership," Bethany agreed. "Please continue."

"So what's my role?" Derek asked a bit too eagerly.

"You've worked with C-4 before, right?" Bishop asked, turning to him.

"Sure, back in my army days. We used it all the time."

Bishop turned to Bethany. "Hailey, show him what you brought."

Bethany nodded and pulled out her duffel bag. She had combined all of the supplies into one sack and she opened it now on top of the blueprints for all to see. "I have fifteen bricks, along with the detonators and timers. We should be good to go." She knew that even though the material was authentic, they would be arresting everyone before the material was actually detonated. Still, a tad of nervousness swept through her. C-4 was dangerous, and no plan, no matter how well thought out, was foolproof.

Although they had made her leave her phone at the

door before this planning session had started, she had a pen in her pocket with an imbedded recording device that was taking down every word. Daniel had a similar device imbedded in his sunglasses in his shirt pocket, just in case her pen device failed. Between the two of them, she knew they would have enough to arrest Liam, Ethan and Derek at a minimum, as well as Bishop. She hoped she could add even more to the count based on Bishop's cell phone contacts and the transcripts from his conversations, but they'd noticed that he'd been making very few calls lately, so they wondered if he'd somehow figured out his phone had been cloned.

For the next ten minutes, Liam went through the details of how to handle the C-4 safely and how to actually set the explosives in the various locations around the stadium. They were going to be breaking into teams of two and working in a grid pattern underneath the major support girders. Then they would set the timers and disappear without rendezvousing later so they wouldn't get caught. After Liam was finished going over the plan, Derek pulled out one of the bricks and acted like he was examining it. "Hey, where did you guys get these? Are you sure it's good quality? This stuff looks pretty cheap to me."

"I have a connection inside the CPD evidence room," Daniel answered. "It's good quality, I'm sure of it. For a fee, the evidence clerk was willing to make sure the C-4 was liberated from the shelves."

Derek raised an eyebrow. "What about these detonators? These are a special type that are hard to find."

Bethany snatched them out of his hand and threw them back in the bag, then zipped it closed. "If you think I'm going to share my sources with the likes of you, you've got another think coming," she said derisively. "All you need to know is that I got them for a good price and they are high quality. I wouldn't cheat the Guard."

Derek obviously didn't like the insult and stepped closer to Bethany in a threatening stance, but Liam and Ethan both saved Daniel from having to step in once again.

"Good grief, Derek," Ethan said tightly. "Can't you meet once without causing a problem?"

"Leave her alone," Liam added.

Bishop went through the rest of the details, including where they would meet the next morning before heading over to the stadium. Once every detail was explained, Bishop handed each of them one of the packs of money they had taken from the armored car heist.

"What's this for?" Liam asked, surprise in his voice. "We don't expect to be paid for our efforts. We're doing this for the Guard."

"After the stadium is destroyed, you'll need to lie low for a while. This money should tide you over until you can show your face again."

"If we disappear, won't that make us look suspicious?" Daniel asked.

"You're complaining?" Derek sneered. "Take the money and be glad the Guard is taking care of you!"

"I'm not complaining," Daniel answered. "I'm just making sure I understand my orders."

"Consider it your lifeboat," Bishop answered. "It's

there if you need it. Hopefully, no one will suspect you and you can go back to work the next day, business as usual. But if problems arise, and you do have a problem and need to disappear, you'll have this to fall back on. If you don't end up needing it, you can always donate it back to the Guard after things settle down. We haven't done anything of this magnitude in quite a long time. We just want to make sure all of our bases are covered."

"We're thankful that you've thought of every contingency in your planning, Bishop," Bethany replied. She put her packet of money in her tote bag. "Hopefully, we won't need this and we can give it back to the Guard, just like you said."

The small group broke up and started to leave.

"Look at that," Bethany whispered quietly in Daniel's ear as they collected their cell phones and guns at the door. Daniel surreptitiously glanced toward Bishop and she hoped he noticed what she had—Bishop had a new cell phone and was making a call from across the room. This one was larger than the old one he had been using and had a dark blue case. No wonder his calls had all but stopped on his old phone.

SIXTEEN

"We need to clone that new phone," she said under her breath as she received her handgun from the man at the door. She kissed Daniel flirtatiously near his ear to cover up what she was saying and gave him a smile and a wink.

He laughed and kissed her back. "Oh, darling, you're amazing," he said out loud. Then quietly for her ears only, he leaned in and said, "Got it, I'll make a diversion. You do the clone."

He stepped away from her and right in the way of Derek, who was swaggering by. "Derek, do you really know how to set a C-4 charge, or are you just filled with hot air?"

Derek puffed out his chest. "I was a specialist in the army. I served overseas in Operation Enduring Freedom," he said roughly. "I know more about setting charges than you've ever dreamed about."

"Can you prove that?" Daniel asked. "I doubt you were even part of that military operation over in Afghanistan." He took a step closer, getting right up into Derek's face. "Could you even recognize an Al-Qaeda soldier if you saw one? Do you know what the Taliban is or what they stand for? You're all about hate, pure and simple. I doubt you actually ever served at all."

Derek's face turned red and spittle spewed from his mouth. "I don't have to prove anything to you," he answered hatefully. "You're just some murdering police scum." His voice started to rise and Liam and Ethan were suddenly on the scene, trying to calm everyone down. Bethany took the opportunity to take a few steps back and pull out her own phone. A few clicks later, the cloning process had begun.

"You do if you expect me to be on the same team with you again," Daniel answered, his voice also rising. "I'm not giving you another opportunity to take a shot at me. I need to know there's really a good reason to have you on that team and that you really do know what you're doing. Were you even listening when Liam was going over the details of how to set the charges? I don't want this mission to fail because of your incompetence."

Derek took both hands and pushed Daniel hard. "There's your reason. Because I say so. Is that good enough for you?"

Daniel scrambled back and threw a punch, landing his fist hard against Derek's chin. He didn't have an opening to throw a second blow, because seconds later, Ethan and Liam had gotten between the two and were once again physically holding them apart.

Bishop was quickly on the scene, as well. His face was serious, and his brow furled. "Are you two going to be able to put aside your differences or not? We're counting on you two to make this happen. This mission is very important to Operation Battlefield. If we can't trust you to do your jobs, we'll have to give them to someone else that we can trust. This isn't a game for children with attitude that put themselves and their personal agenda before the Guard."

Daniel pulled against Liam's grip, but relaxed once he got the signal from Bethany that the cloning was complete. "It was my fault. I'm sorry. I let my anger get the best of me. It won't happen again." Liam released him and he took a step away from Derek, putting his hands up in a motion of surrender. "You can count on me. I'm all in."

He took Bethany's hand, gave her a kiss on the cheek and hugged her close.

"We're committed to the cause, Bishop. Both of us," Bethany reassured him. "And we'll be there tomorrow morning. You can count on us." She watched the worry lines slowly disappear from his face.

"Alright, Hailey. We're putting a lot of faith in you to get this job done."

The two left the building and quickly got into Daniel's truck and drove away from the warehouse where the meeting had been held.

Bethany immediately started reading through Bishop's cloned texts and data as Daniel drove. "Anything interesting on that phone?" Daniel asked.

She kept scrolling. "He refers to a phase one and phase two a couple of times. It makes me think that the stadium demolition is only part of Operation Battlefield, like he mentioned today, but what could phase two be? And really, what's the point of killing all of those people at the stadium? I don't understand the reasoning behind it. There has to be something else going on that we haven't figured out yet. It has to be a piece of a bigger plan."

Daniel glanced over at her. "Well, we'd better figure it out soon since this whole thing is supposed to go down tomorrow. Let's pull Captain Murphy and Agent Hooker in and see if they have any ideas. We need help with the research." He turned a corner. "Do you see anything about Derek in those texts? I still can't understand why they brought him back into the fold. That guy is a menace and a problem just waiting to happen."

"No, and their decision to do so makes me nervous. It's not a wise move on their part and they're usually smarter than that. They have to see that decision raises big red flags."

Bethany kept scrolling. "It makes me think they've got something planned for him, like making him a scapegoat for the stadium tomorrow." She looked over at Daniel, who kept checking his mirrors. "Anybody following us?"

"Nobody so far. I'm keeping an eye out though." He checked again, made several turns and lane changes but drove carefully, presumably so Bethany wouldn't get sick this time. She smiled at him, appreciating his efforts.

"Wow, your driving has really improved. I'm impressed."

He laughed and she saw the dimple appear on his

left cheek. "Well, I was rewarded for my efforts with a kiss the last time. I'm hoping to be rewarded again."

Her own cheeks burned as she remembered the kiss they had shared right before Captain Murphy had arrived to give them the C-4 they needed for the operation. She had to admit, it had felt good to be held in Daniel's arms. They had been stealing kisses and touches frequently when they were around the Guard, but that had been for the benefit of the roles they were playing. Or had it been? At first, it had been hard for her to receive the small intimacies, but now she was slowly not only accepting them but actually looking forward to them. She liked holding hands and the gentle caresses he offered without being pushy or demanding. He seemed to know when to come close and when to give her some space. It was uncanny. Just knowing he was nearby had once made her nervous and jumpy, but was now giving her comfort and making her feel whole and complete.

She stole a look at him from the corner of her eye. At first, she had dreaded this assignment. Daniel was untested in the field and had never done any undercover work, but she also had to admit that he was doing his job well. He had fit in with the others and so far had played his role without gaffs or rookie mistakes. But there was more to it than that. She could tell that he was looking out for her, and that he really cared about her. She felt…*cherished.*

But could she trust him? Her old boyfriend had cared about her too, or at least he had said he did. He had said and done all the right things at just the right times too. And then the next thing she knew, she found him in the arms of another woman and was utterly humiliated in front of all of her friends and coworkers. She had thought she knew him, but he had publicly shattered her trust. Could she ever trust again? Was it worth the pain if she was wrong?

She stole another look at Daniel as he kept his eyes on the road. She was attracted to more than just his good looks, but she also knew for a fact that he wasn't willing to share his past with her, and it hurt to know that he wasn't willing to open up to her about his family. She didn't think he would ever be so cruel as to make promises to her and then be unfaithful. Daniel was too loyal, too considerate to treat anyone that way. He would never intentionally hurt her. But she didn't think he would voluntarily tell her about his private life either, and she didn't think it was right to try to force him to reveal his secrets. The problem was, if he was hiding his past, what else would he hide from her? What other parts of his life would he keep secret? She would always be wondering. There would be no trust. And the relationship would inevitably suffer.

Her stomach twisted in knots as the realization of the depth of her feelings overtook her. She loved him. That made it even harder. She hadn't wanted to admit it, but she could no longer push those feelings aside. But could she compromise? Even though she cared for Daniel, she didn't think she could. She didn't want to love him, especially when there didn't seem to be any future for their relationship, but she couldn't help herself. It was a good thing this mission was almost over.

Tomorrow they would make the arrests at the stadium and then Operation Battlefield would be over, and they would go their separate ways. She would take her new FBI assignment and move to a new city, putting Chattanooga and Daniel far behind her.

She wondered fleetingly what her options would be. Miami? New York City? Or maybe a smaller city in a rural area? Why didn't the prospect of moving on fill her with excitement the way she would have expected?

She knew it was time to pray. God was always her strength in difficult times. If there were ever a time to seek His guidance, it was now. She poured out her heart in her prayer, as well as her fears about what the future would bring. She also prayed for protection for both herself and Daniel as they entered this most dangerous part of their undercover mission.

Her FBI phone suddenly rang, bringing her back to the present. She looked at the number and identified it as the new number that Hooker had supplied.

"Yes, sir? This is Hailey." These days, she always used her undercover name, just in case the phone was compromised in any way. It also made it easier to stay in character if she always answered with her undercover name.

She listened for a while, then answered. "Yes, sir. Thank you for the information." Then she told her FBI boss about what had happened during the meeting and the plans for the stadium. She also told him where he could pick up the pen and glasses that had recorded the meeting that morning, and their need to research and figure out the rest of Operation Battlefield. A few minutes later, the call ended and she stored her phone again.

"Everything okay?" Daniel asked.

"Not really," she answered. "The FBI has found incontrovertible proof that Max Westfield was intercepting all of the communication between us and Special Agent Hooker. That's why we weren't able to contact him. They've found evidence that Max was tampering with the Heritage Guard files, as well. He was definitely the mole and was probably also behind Justin's death. They're trying to tie him to it as we speak. And now, Max Westfield has disappeared."

SEVENTEEN

Daniel stood guard as Bethany pressed the C-4 into the crevice between the two girders at the stadium, his hand on the butt of his pistol. They were alone in the shadows and it was about noon, although people were scattered throughout the stadium, working and setting up for the afternoon festivities. Several bands had already arrived and were warming up in different areas around the field and out in the parking lot. Workers were manning the concession areas, as well as the ticket booths and the top deck where the officials who would be judging the event had congregated.

Although they were still playing a role, there was no way the stadium would actually explode—that is, if law enforcement had anything to say about it. Bethany and Daniel had met with a joint FBI and Chattanooga Police Department task force yesterday after their Guard meeting and filled them in on all the details, so there were plenty of plain-clothed officers on the scene ready to make the arrests once they got the word to do so. The law enforcement teams were all connected by radio and were checking in on a regular basis. Until they knew the rest of the plans for Operation Battlefield, however, the FBI wanted to continue going through the motions as if the stadium explosion would still go on as planned. It was the hope that either the research team would discover a connection between some of Bishop's texts and some other bit of news, or that Bishop or one of the other Guard members would let something slip in the moments leading up to the explosion that would give the rest of the Guard's plans away.

Daniel hummed along to the loud speaker that was playing Christmas music from a local radio station. The tune just added to the cacophony of sounds echoing off the walls of concrete, but he could still hear the law enforcement announcements through the speaker in his ear, as well. Every once in a while, the DJ would come on and announce a current event that was planned for the upcoming weekend in Chattanooga, but there really didn't seem to be much going on besides the normal holiday and charity galas that happened every year. Bethany and Daniel had been sure to report what they had discovered on Bishop's phone about the phase one and phase two events and their theories, but it was hard to pinpoint anything that would have garnered the attention of the Guard as being worthy of a phase two event. Nothing scheduled in Chattanooga or the surrounding area over the next few weeks seemed to be noteworthy enough. However, agents and officers were still scrambling to come up with anything that might fit the Heritage Guard agenda.

What added to the frustration was the fact that there

was no hard evidence against anyone in the Guard organization who ranked above Bishop Jacobs to prove the conspiracy. They had a few vague texts, and a few names, but nothing concrete. The Heritage Guard had also only used a small amount of the stolen money on the C-4 they had purchased. The Guard was still planning something bigger. They just didn't know what that bigger picture could be.

Daniel spoke into his microphone attached to his sleeve. "All clear at checkpoint delta." He turned to Bethany, who was still listening in on Bishop's phone with a small earpiece. "How's it going?"

"I'm almost done," Bethany replied.

"That's good," Westfield answered, stepping out of the shadows. "I was afraid you wouldn't follow through on your task for the Guard."

Daniel was quick to unholster his weapon and point it at Westfield, but the rogue FBI man was quicker. He also had a silencer on the end of his weapon, so when he fired his shot at Daniel, nobody heard the bullet that hit Daniel in the arm above the wrist and tore the skin as it skirted toward his elbow. Daniel dropped his gun, unable to keep his grip or even hit the button on his microphone to notify the other law enforcement officers due to the pain.

"Max, no!" Bethany yelled. She went for him as if to tackle him, but he instantly swung the gun in her direction and she stopped short, apparently realizing that she couldn't stop him without getting shot herself.

"Keep your voice down, and no sudden moves, either of you. I will kill you, Bethany. I won't enjoy it, but I'll do it." He looked behind him to make sure no one had noticed their activities, but they were still alone in the shadows.

Daniel grabbed his wounded right arm, trying to staunch the flow of blood. His arm felt like it was on fire, and he pressed the fabric from his shirt and coat against the wound, hoping the pressure would help stop the bleeding. He gritted his teeth, angry that Westfield had been able to sneak up on them without his noticing.

"Put your guns on the floor, now," Westfield ordered, pointing his weapon at Bethany. "You too, Daniel. I know you carry a second piece. And pull out that microphone you have up your sleeve and your phones." Bethany complied, pulling her service pistol from her waistband as well as her small derringer from her boot. She slowly added her cell phone to the pile growing at her feet. Daniel also gave up his second gun, his phone, and the microphone. Westfield collected the weapons and secured them in the pockets of his coat, then crushed the rest with the heel of his boot. Then he forced them up against the concrete wall of the stadium and frisked them. When he came to Bethany, his hands were overly friendly and Bethany kicked him hard in response.

Westfield's face turned red and he grabbed Bethany's hair, hard, obviously hurting her and causing her to gasp. "It must have escaped your attention that I'm in charge now. Try that again and I'll shoot you right here and now." He pushed her against the concrete so roughly that her head hit the corner edge, causing a scrape and a line of blood to form on her temple.

Westfield smiled when he saw the wound and the blood start to trickle down her face. "Now you have a gift to remember me by." He finished frisking her, found Bethany's knife in her boot and confiscated that, as well.

"Any other hardware I should know about?"

She shook her head but didn't verbally respond. Her eyes were burning with fire. Daniel couldn't help thinking that Westfield was an idiot. If he thought his rough treatment of Bethany was going to subdue her, the result was actually the opposite. Bethany was now fighting mad.

"So you're a member of the Heritage Guard?" Daniel asked, his voice filled with derision.

Westfield laughed. "Look who just caught up."

"Which means you killed Justin," Bethany added.

He shrugged. "He was unfortunate collateral damage. I actually liked the man, but he couldn't be swayed."

"Collateral damage?" Bethany said coldly, trembling with anger. "He was a person, with a family and friends. You act as if his death meant nothing at all."

Westfield shrugged. "He got in our way." He took a few steps to the left and quickly looked behind himself, making sure they were still truly alone. Once satisfied, he returned his attention to his quarry in front of him. "The Guard has known about you for a couple of months now, Bethany, and has been using you and your abilities to advance our agenda. You've been able to provide us with quite a lot of valuable commodities—not to mention the fact that you make a very talented armed robber." He gave her a chilling smile. "I have to admit, it took us a while to figure out that you were the one who had infiltrated our group. We knew someone had because the FBI kept thwarting our plans, but we didn't know it was you until I joined the FBI myself and got access to the files."

"The FBI does thorough background checks before hiring anyone," Bethany said defiantly. "How did you manage to hide your connection to the Heritage Guard?"

Westfield smiled. "I had references from powerful people in high places, not to mention computer specialists working for the Guard who smoothed over any questions about my qualifications. Not a single red flag appeared. The Guard is not without resources, Bethany. You should know that. We have friends everywhere." He leaned closer. "Instead of worrying about me though, you should really be worrying about yourself." He shifted, but kept his weapon trained on both of them. "We thought about killing you outright but figured the FBI would just send in another agent. That's why we decided to take out Justin instead. By taking out the head of the snake, we figured that would kill the investigation. We didn't realize you would keep pushing so hard to keep the mission going, or that the FBI would listen and let you stay involved with the Guard. We were able to make sure you didn't get too much intelligence, but now the time has come for you and your boyfriend here to be eliminated, as well." He smiled again, a smirk that made Daniel's blood boil. "Don't worry though. Once the stadium blows up, we'll be sure to verify that you and Daniel, along with the FBI and the Chattanooga Police Department, get all the credit for the explosion. They'll find your bodies here in the rubble, along with your fingerprints all over the materials. Plus, they'll be able to trace the materials back to the CPD evidence locker, which will further prove your involvement."

"You won't get away with it," Bethany said fervently under her breath. "You may think you've won, but even if we die today, others will stop you."

"*If* you die today?" Westfield laughed. "Darling, that's an *absolute certainty.*" He took a step closer and ran his hand suggestively down her cheek. "And won't it prove interesting when they find out that you were also in on the bank robbery and on that armored car heist. It will add even more fuel to the fire when they find money that was stolen from the armored car back in your apartment. Yes, the FBI will be kept quite busy defending you and its actions. We've thought of everything. Let me assure you—you'll be quite the news story. Now turn around and finish setting that explosive properly."

It was all Daniel could do not to pounce on Westfield and shove the gun down his throat. He couldn't stand seeing him touch Bethany, especially in such a personal manner. But he could also see the message in her eyes. *Wait. Watch.* There would be a better opportunity to strike. Right now, Westfield held all the cards. He was too close to them with his loaded gun, and if either of them tried something, one or both of them could end up dead. No, the smart move was to wait, just as her wordless missive was suggesting.

Bethany turned and continued working on the explosive, but she kept the conversation going. "Well if you're so convinced, Westfield, there's no harm in telling us the rest of the Operation Battlefield plan. We've been trying to figure it out all morning. Phase one is blowing up the stadium. What is phase two?"

Westfield was silent for a moment, as if considering the situation, and Daniel wasn't sure if he was going to answer. Then the hubris got the better of him and the words spilled from his mouth. "Well, I guess there's no harm in telling you since you'll be dead soon anyway." He started to pace, yet kept the gun trained on their midriffs. It was almost as if he were dancing to the Christmas music that was playing in the background.

"The governor is hosting a Christmas party tonight, and has invited several dignitaries, including both senators from Tennessee and three of our nine federal representatives. Unfortunately, some of the food at the party is going to be tainted, and a lot of the people are going to get sick. Some of the people are even going to die—including the three congressmen and two senators. It will all look like a terrible accident, but no one will really care, because everyone will be talking about the horrible bomb that took out the stadium and all of those dear children at the marching band competition. The entire focus will be on the corruption within the FBI and the CPD and how they could allow a joint operation to go so terribly wrong. In the meantime, new senators and congressmen will need to be appointed to finish out the terms of the people who accidentally died at the party. While the nation hones in on the stadium tragedy, the Heritage Guard has people in place to make sure Guard members are selected to fill those empty spots in the federal government with little to no opposition.".

Bethany stopped her work and glared at Westfield. "All of those people sick or murdered, just to advance the Guard's agenda. There are other ways to reach your objectives without all the killing."

"You make think so, my dear, but with five new members of congress pushing the Guard's agenda at the federal level, amazing things can happen, and we just don't have time to wait." He shifted. "And don't start believing that the Guard has a limited influence only in the tiny little state of Tennessee. We're growing every day. This is just the beginning. The Heritage Guard has a glorious future. We'll be moving mountains in no time."

He pulled some rope out of one of the pockets of his jacket and threw it on the ground in front of Bethany. "Tie him up. Tightly. And believe me, I'm going to check, so do a good job."

Bethany picked up the rope and turned to Daniel. She met his eye and he saw worry and love radiating back at him. *Love?* Wait, was that really love there? He was so excited to see the emotion there written on her face it almost made him forget that a madman was standing a few feet away, pointing a deadly weapon at them.

"How is your arm?" she asked softly.

"I think it's the least of our problems right now." He put his hands up, and she tied them together.

"Now, sit and tie his feet," Westfield ordered. "And add this gag," he said, throwing a bandanna on the ground.

They complied, and once Daniel was incapacitated, Westfield pocketed his gun and faced Bethany with a length of rope. "Put your hands together. Now."

Bethany complied, but then at the last minute, she struck out with her fist and caught Westfield in the chin. The traitor had been expecting defiance, however, and the blow didn't hit with the full force that Bethany had intended. Westfield countered with a hit to Bethany's gut that took her breath away. He was then able to grab her left arm and wrench it behind her, causing her to cry out in pain. She struggled against him and Daniel writhed against his bindings and bit against the gag, frustrated by his lack of ability to help.

Westfield pulled even harder against Bethany's arm, yanking it so roughly she cried out again. He pushed her against the wall, forcing her face against the cold gray concrete and pulling her arm up her back in an awkward angle so she could barely move without being in severe pain. "Keep fighting me, Bethany, and I'll break your arm, I swear I will."

She finally quit fighting and nodded. "Okay, Westfield. You win."

He released her arm and flipped her around so he was seeing her face-to-face. "I didn't want it to end this way between us. I really didn't. I wanted us to be on the same side. We could have been so good together, you and me. We could have made an excellent team."

"I would never join you," Bethany said, her voice full of derision. "You disgust me."

It was apparently the wrong thing to say. Westfield's eyes turned cold, and he brought his fist back and slammed it into Bethany's face. Her head bounced against the concrete behind her, and her body went limp and fell to the ground.

Daniel yelled, but the gag kept him from making any real sound. He tried to kick out at Westfield, but being trussed up like a Christmas turkey made it hard for him to do much, and Westfield ended up giving him two hard kicks in the gut in response and pushed him away. As Daniel tried to regain his breath, Westfield tied Bethany up and left her in a heap in the corner.

Then he stood over both of them and laughed.

"Relax, Daniel. You're about to be famous. And don't forget, it's for a good cause."

With that, he checked the explosives to verify that they were set properly, then turned and left, sauntering down the stadium walkway, leaving them with the C-4 and the detonator set, the timer silently counting off the minutes before the explosion would rock the stadium and take out the entire south wall.

EIGHTEEN

Bethany's head was pounding. Was that a bass drum playing in her brain? Why wouldn't it stop? She tried to sit up, but the pounding got worse.

"Bethany? Lie still. You might have a concussion."

"Daniel?" Her mind was a bit foggy. She remembered… Suddenly, it all came rushing back to her and she opened her eyes at the same time that she tried to move her arms and legs.

"How long was I out?"

"Only a few minutes."

Her hands were tied behind her and her feet were bound together, both rather securely with lengths of white rope that Westfield had brought with him. She looked over at Daniel. He had apparently bitten through the thin bandanna that Westfield had used to gag him and was now working on trying to loosen the ropes on his own hands and feet. He actually looked like he was having a bit of success, and Bethany had to admit that she was impressed. Westfield had checked her knots when he had forced her to tie Daniel up. He was bound securely.

"I can't believe you're getting out of those ropes. How are you managing it?"

Daniel was silent for a moment as if contemplating his answer, then finally swallowed heavily. "Unfortunately, I've had some experience with escaping difficult situations like this. My brother used to tie me up for fun when I was younger. It was a game to him and his friends. They would tie me up in knots with rope or whatever they could find and then leave me that way for hours. I got pretty good at getting untied. I had lots of chances to hone my skills."

Bethany looked at him, sure that her wide eyes were reflecting the shock and disgust she was feeling. How could a brother do such a thing? Especially an older brother who should have been protecting a younger one from an abusive parent? Still, she made sure to keep her voice level and calm. She knew instinctively that pity was not what Daniel would want to hear—now or ever. "How long did they leave you like that?"

Daniel kept working on the ropes as he spoke and didn't meet her eyes. "At first, it was only for a few minutes at a time. I was six or so. Then it stretched into longer periods because they lost interest and forgot about me. A couple of times, I was stuck like that for almost twenty-four hours."

"Oh, Daniel," Bethany muttered. Still, she was pleased that he had shared part of his past with her, even if it was a series of horrific memories from his childhood. He had actually told her something about his family, and she could tell that even though it had been difficult for him, he was glad that he had done so.

"Yeah, well, like I said, I've had a little practice at getting out of tight situations, and that might actually come in handy right about now." He grimaced. "I apologize in advance. I'm about to do something and, well, this sound might bother you."

She heard a *pop* and he winced as his shoulder went out of joint, but that movement made the rope just slack enough around his wrists that he was able to pull at the bindings and release the rope from around his hands and free himself. He popped the joint back in place, then untied his feet, moving a little slowly because of his injured arm.

"Tell me you did not just pop your shoulder out of the joint so you could free yourself," she said softly, wincing as she imagined the pain that must be associated with such a maneuver.

"It hurt a lot worse the first time it happened, believe me."

She raised an eyebrow. "And now?"

"It makes my arm sore for a while, but I don't really notice it anymore."

There was quite a bit of blood on the rope near his wrists and on his coat and shirt where he had been bleeding from the bullet wound, but he seemed to be ignoring that as well, as he turned his focus to untying Bethany's bindings. Once he had her free, he gently cupped her head in his hands and kissed her on the lips.

"I love you, Bethany. I'm so sorry that Westfield hurt you."

It was a wonderful kiss, sweet and full of promise.

"I'm sorry about your brother," she said softly. "Thank you for telling me."

"Yeah, well, you wanted the unvarnished truth. That's one reason why I don't send him Christmas cards every year. We've never been close. He's six years older than me, and he had a different father, so when my mom started losing it, she sent him to live with his old man. I haven't heard from him since."

"Did he know you were being abused growing up?"

"I don't know what he knew or didn't know. Frankly, once he was gone, it was just one less problem I had to deal with. If he did know, I don't think he cared." He gently wiped the blood off the cut on her temple where Westfield had bashed her against the concrete wall.

"We only have a few minutes until this C-4 is set to blow. Do you know how to disarm it?" Daniel asked.

"Sure. That's the easy part. Then we need to get through to the rest of the stadium and make sure all of the rest of the C-4 is disarmed, as well. Who knows how far Westfield has gotten or if law enforcement had any trouble making the arrests."

"He smashed both of our cell phones and the radio," Daniel said, his tone matter-of-fact, "but we'll get Westfield and a status report. This place is loaded with law enforcement. I'm actually surprised no one has come up here to check on us." He stood and examined the charges. "Can you tell me how to do it? The timer says we have eight minutes left before this is set to blow."

Bethany shook her head, then regretted it when the pain got worse because of the movement. She gritted her teeth and started to stand, and Daniel grabbed her hand with his uninjured arm and helped pull her to her feet.

"I'll take care of it." She quickly disarmed the bomb and removed the C-4, detonator and timer from the girder. Once she was sure they were safe, she secured all of the material into different compartments of her coat. Then they left the secluded area and immediately headed for the lower area of the stadium where the concessions and more populated sections were located. All they needed to do was find someone in law enforcement before they ran into someone from the Heritage Guard.

Unfortunately, Derek was the next face they came across, and he was quick to whip out his gun and point it directly at Daniel and Bethany.

"Well, if it isn't the two traitors I was looking for," he said, a sneer in his voice.

"What are you talking about?" Daniel asked, immediately putting his hands up while at the same time moving in a protective stance in front of Bethany.

Bethany would have objected—she was usually able to take care of herself, thank you, but her head was still not right after Westfield had bounced it off the concrete. She did know this—it didn't make sense that Derek was still in the stadium and running around with a loaded weapon. He should have been arrested with the rest of the Guard members. Hopefully, law enforcement had already made sure that all of the other charges had been disarmed throughout the stadium, but if Derek was still free, then maybe the stadium was still in jeopardy and all the people were still in harm's way after all. A nervous knot tightened in her stomach as she glanced at her watch. "What are you doing here?" she asked. "You were supposed to set your charges and clear out like the rest of us."

"Bishop told us all that you two had betrayed the Guard. He sent me up here to deal with both of you."

Daniel took a step forward. "Really? Well, let's just think about this. The timers are set to go off in less than five minutes. If what you say is true, then it sounds to me like he sent you up here to die, don't you think?" As he spoke, he got closer and closer to Derek, until he suddenly reached with his good arm and grabbed for the gun, forcing it up so the barrel was pointed toward the ceiling. It fired, the noise echoing off the concrete walls as the two men struggled for supremacy of the loaded weapon. The bullet ricocheted away and zinged against walls as the two men wrestled.

Daniel tried to wrench the gun away, but Derek's grip was tighter than he'd thought and he only had one good arm to fight with. Without realizing it, Derek hit Daniel's bad arm where the bullet wound injury was fresh. Daniel grunted and quickly kicked Derek's knee in response and the man's leg collapsed. Derek shrieked in pain and when he fell to the left, Daniel hit him hard in the stomach with his good arm and then again with his knee. Derek coughed in response and released the gun, then fell to the ground and grabbed his injured knee with both hands, writhing. "I think you broke my leg!" he spat, as he rolled back and forth.

Daniel ignored him and kick him again, making

sure he wasn't getting up again any time soon, and also ensuring that he wouldn't try anything while he was down. Bethany was quickly there, frisking him for weapons. She found his phone and immediately called their law enforcement contact to find out the status of the bombs in the stadium while Daniel kept the weapon trained on Derek's midriff. "Don't move a muscle, Derek."

"We're clear," Bethany said, visibly relieved. She blew out a breath, and closed her eyes for a moment, then opened them again. "The other thirteen bricks of C-4 have been accounted for. They've arrested Liam, Bishop, Ethan and two others from the Guard that Bishop must have called in to assist."

Two security guards suddenly appeared on the scene, their weapons drawn, apparently coming to check out the source of the gunshot.

"CPD," Daniel announced, as they approached. "This man is a perp and needs to be taken into custody." To his credit, Derek kept his mouth shut, even as the two guards arrested him and handcuffed him. Daniel was glad Derek was done fighting. He didn't have much strength left in his hand that was holding the gun, but he didn't have time to stop and get medical treatment either. They needed to stop Westfield and the Guard before they hurt the congressmen at the Christmas party.

Bethany came to his side and touched his arm gently. "Are you okay?"

He looked into her eyes, and could tell that she was asking about more than just his physical condition. He thought about what he had told her about his brother's abuse. He hadn't planned to share that with her—but he hadn't stopped himself either. He had never shared that story with anybody before and hadn't known exactly what kind of reaction to expect, but afterward he was glad that he had told her about his brother's behavior. She wanted to know the true story of his past, and it had actually felt good to tell her.

"I will be," he answered softly. He holstered his gun and took her hand. "Let's go stop the Guard from doing any more damage." He looked down at their entwined fingers and smiled.

The difference was the love, he realized. Although she hadn't said the words, he had seen it in her face and mirrored in her eyes. He knew her feelings for him were growing and were stronger than they ever had been. He was patient. Their relationship had strengthened over the last few days, and he had seen changes in Bethany that he hadn't seen even when they had been dating the year before.

There were changes in him too, he realized. Before, he hadn't wanted to tell her about his life growing up, but now he had taken the plunge and decided that it was worth the sacrifice. He wanted Bethany in his life. Period. If that meant he needed to tell her every detail of his past, then he would do it. He loved her. He would do whatever it took to make sure they could be together. He wasn't going to blurt it all out in one sitting, but little by little, he was finally willing to share that part of himself with her—only with her.

Thank you, Lord, for giving me the strength to share

my past with Bethany. I've buried the pain inside for so long that I didn't think it was possible to talk about it out loud, but You've helped me see that it's not only possible, but necessary so I can move on and deal with my past. Thank You for bringing her back into my life and giving us a second chance.

NINETEEN

"Freeze, Westfield," Daniel said, his voice cold and clear. His weapon was unwavering as he pointed it at Westfield's head. The man was sitting in a chair in a small private airfield's lobby, waiting for the small jet he'd hired to whisk him away into obscurity. Thankfully, Daniel and Bethany had been able to track Westfield down through internet purchases a mere twenty minutes before the plane was set to take off, despite the man's attempts to stay hidden and escape.

"I wouldn't do that," Bethany said, as Max turned slightly as if he were going to either close his laptop or push some of the buttons on the computer. She also had her weapon drawn and was coming at him from the opposite doorway.

"Ah, Bethany. I'm so glad you came to see me off." He smiled, but it was a sad smile, as if they shared some secret together.

"I'm sure you've heard by now that the stadium was saved," she said quietly. "None of the C-4 charges detonated and no one was hurt." She took a step closer.

"The governor's Christmas party also got canceled. The food is being tested as we speak. Anything tainted will be destroyed before it can harm anyone, and whoever poisoned it will be prosecuted. Operation Battlefield has failed, Westfield. Both phase one and phase two were a complete wash."

Westfield shrugged. "You'll undoubtedly arrest a few, but the Heritage Guard operates in cells for a reason. You won't be able to get at the true leaders. They're too deeply hidden—too entrenched for you to find them. The Guard will live on and will rise again."

"That's what we thought too, until we found the hidden hard drives in the dry cleaners when we did a very thorough search of the place about an hour ago. Our search warrant pretty much let us tear the place apart, and you'd be surprised at the membership lists we found, not to mention the financial records, offshore accounts and other valuable information we discovered. The attorney general and local state attorney are going to be delivering a joint statement within a few hours, and will be issuing subpoenas and indictments on a national scale. This case is huge. The Heritage Guard is finished."

Bethany took another step closer. "What did you say to us when we were in the stadium all tied up? Oh, yeah, you're gonna be famous!" She pulled out her handcuffs. "Now set down that computer, stand up and put your hands behind your back."

He slowly set the computer aside and stood, but then he quickly put something in his mouth and then held his hands up and closed his eyes.

"No!" Both Daniel and Bethany yelled it in unison, holstered their weapons and tried to get the substance out of his mouth, but he clamped his jaws together and wouldn't open them. Within a few short moments, white foam started to ooze out between his lips and his body started to convulse. He fell to the ground, and Daniel kept trying to save him while Bethany pulled out her radio and called an ambulance for help. The faint smell of almonds hung in the air.

"I need an emergency bus for a suspected cyanide poisoning," she said hurriedly, and rattled off the address.

"He's seizing," Daniel said. "He's already unconscious and his pulse is weak. They're not going to make it here in time."

Bethany felt in Westfield's pocket and found a small empty packet. "He must have had this on him just in case he was captured." She looked at his face that was already pale. "He chose the coward's way out." She stood, disgust and anger warring on her face. She kicked a chair, sending it flying across the room. "I didn't want him dead! I wanted him in prison, but not dead!"

"He made the choice," Daniel said, feeling for a pulse. "You didn't kill him. He did this to himself." He stood, pulled out a handkerchief from his pocket and wiped his hands. "He's gone."

EPILOGUE

Daniel paced back and forth outside of the entrance to Rock City on Lookout Mountain, Georgia, just on the outskirts of Chattanooga. It had been almost three weeks since the big arrests from the Heritage Guard had come down, yet the case was still making huge headlines and being discussed on the nightly news on a regular basis. Christmas had come and gone, but he had barely had a chance to celebrate or spend time with Bethany because she had been so busy at the FBI with follow-up work from the case. His reputation and personal records had all been restored, and he had returned to his normal work at the Chattanooga Police Department, but he really missed working with Bethany side by side as they had on the Heritage Guard case. Today, she had asked for him to meet her here, but he had a sinking feeling that she was meeting him today only to say goodbye. It was a bitter pill to swallow.

She had succeeded professionally beyond her wildest dreams, and he was sure that the FBI was going to offer her the assignment of her choice once things settled down at the bureau. Where would she go? California? New York City? The thought of losing her hung over his head like a huge storm cloud, ready to thunder and let loose a deluge of rain.

She had never told him she loved him. It weighed heavily upon him. He had blurted out bits and pieces of his past and told her his feelings, but it obviously hadn't convinced her to stay. He'd thought he'd done enough to get her trust him, but apparently, he hadn't. He'd failed, and now she was going to break his heart for good.

At least she was going to meet him and say good-bye. The last time, she had disappeared without a trace.

His heart felt like a stone in his chest and the pain seemed to radiate out and seep into every other part of his body.

He paced some more and watched in trepidation as he saw her pull her car into the parking lot, park and approach. She was wearing jeans, a red sweater and a blue coat that brought out the color in her cheeks and made her face look radiant. She smiled and gave him a quick kiss on the cheek.

"Sorry, I'm a tad late. There was a car accident at the bottom of the mountain and the police are rerouting folks around it."

He ran his hands through his hair. "I hope nobody was hurt."

She shook her head. "I don't think so. Looked like a fender bender." She reached over and gently touched his nose. "Hey, that's really healing up nicely."

He laughed nervously. "Yeah, although I think it will be crooked for life. It's a little souvenir of the Heri-

tage Guard case that I'll get to keep with me forever."
He took her hand and squeezed it, then tensely walked
to the ticket booth. They bought tickets and together
they entered the attraction. It was a beautiful day, and
even though it was chilly, the sky was sunny and blue
and they could see for miles from the bridges and over-
look. Daniel was secretly glad that there weren't many
other people around, and they basically had the beautiful location to themselves.

Daniel wanted to start a conversation, but he was so
worried that today was the last time that he was going
to see her that he didn't even know how to begin.

Bethany must have sensed his nervousness. She
squeezed his hand. "I'm really glad you were available to meet today. I'm sorry I've been so out of pocket.
I've missed you."

Daniel stopped walking and looked her straight in
the eye. He took his free hand and gently touched her
cheek. "I've missed you too."

They started walking again, then Daniel suddenly
stopped and took both her hands. "Okay, I can't take
it anymore. Are you here to say goodbye? Just tell me
now, okay? I mean, I'm glad you didn't just disappear
without telling me, but—"

She stopped him with a kiss. He took a step back,
surprised, but didn't break the kiss.

She took a step closer and twined her hands around
his neck.

When the kiss finally ended, he pulled her close and
whispered in her ear. "That was a wonderful goodbye kiss."

She pulled back. "Who said I'm saying goodbye?"

A small seed of hope was planted in his chest. Maybe God truly was the God of second chances, and had granted him a second chance with Bethany. He looked into her eye and saw—dare he hope—love reflected back at him. But would she say the words? "With all of your success at the FBI, I thought they would probably give you your choice of assignments."

"They did."

"Well, what did you choose?"

She smiled. "They offered me a promotion right here in Chattanooga, so I took it."

He hugged her close. "I thought you would take New York, or something more exotic."

"Why would I do that?" she asked. She pulled back so she could see his face again and cupped his cheeks in her hands. "I love you, Daniel Morley. And I'm not going anywhere."

* * * * *

Don't miss Kathleen Tailer's next thrilling novel,
Perilous Pursuit

Available June 2019 wherever
Love Inspired Suspense books
and ebooks are sold.

Get 4 FREE REWARDS!

We'll send you 2 FREE Books plus 2 FREE Mystery Gifts.

Love Inspired® Suspense books feature Christian characters facing challenges to their faith... and lives.

FREE Value Over $20

SPECIAL EXCERPT FROM

Love Inspired
SUSPENSE

*A K-9 cop must keep his childhood friend alive
when she finds herself in the crosshairs of a
drug-smuggling operation.*

Read on for a sneak preview of
Act of Valor *by Dana Mentink,*
the next exciting installment in the
True Blue K-9 Unit *miniseries, available in May 2019
from Love Inspired Suspense.*

Officer Zach Jameson surveyed the throng of people congregated around the ticket counter at LaGuardia Airport. Most ignored Zach and K-9 partner, Eddie, and that suited him just fine. Two months earlier he would have greeted people with a smile, or at least a polite nod while he and Eddie did their work of scanning for potential drug smugglers. These days he struggled to keep his mind on his duty while the ever-present darkness nibbled at the edges of his soul.

Eddie plopped himself on Zach's boot. He stroked the dog's ears, trying to clear away the fog that had descended the moment he heard of his brother's death.

Zach hadn't had so much as a whiff of suspicion that his brother was in danger. His brain knew he should talk to somebody, somebody like Violet Griffin, his friend from childhood who'd reached out so many times, but his heart would not let him pass through the dark curtain.

"Just get to work," he muttered to himself as his phone rang. He checked the number.

Violet.

He considered ignoring it, but Violet didn't ever call unless she needed help, and she rarely needed anyone. Strong enough to run a ticket counter at LaGuardia and have enough energy left over to help out at Griffin's, her family's diner. She could handle belligerent customers in both arenas and bake the best apple pie he'd ever had the privilege to chow down.

It almost made him smile as he accepted the call.

"Someone's after me, Zach."

Panic rippled through their connection. Panic, from a woman who was tough as they came. "Who? Where are you?"

Her breath was shallow as if she was running.

"I'm trying to get to the break room. I can lock myself in, but I don't… I can't…" There was a clatter.

"Violet?" he shouted.

But there was no answer.

Don't miss
Act of Valor *by Dana Mentink,*
available May 2019 wherever
Love Inspired® Suspense books and ebooks are sold.

www.LoveInspired.com

Looking for inspiration in tales
of hope, faith and heartfelt romance?

Check out **Love Inspired®** and
Love Inspired® Suspense books!

New books available every month!

CONNECT WITH US AT:

Facebook.com/groups/HarlequinConnection

Facebook.com/HarlequinBooks

Twitter.com/HarlequinBooks

Instagram.com/HarlequinBooks

Pinterest.com/HarlequinBooks

ReaderService.com

SPECIAL EXCERPT FROM

Love Inspired®

When a young Amish man needs help finding a wife, his beautiful matchmaker agrees to give him dating lessons...

Read on for a sneak preview of
A Perfect Amish Match *by Vannetta Chapman, available May 2019 from Love Inspired!*

"Dating is so complicated."

"People are complicated, Noah. Every single person you meet is dealing with something."

He asked, "How did you get so wise?"

"Never said I was."

"I'm being serious. How did you learn to navigate so seamlessly through these kinds of interactions, and why aren't you married?"

Olivia Mae thought her eyes were going to pop out of her head. "Did you really just ask me that?"

"I did."

"A little intrusive."

"Meaning you don't want to answer?"

"Meaning it's none of your business."

"Fair enough, though it's like asking a horse salesman why he doesn't own a horse."

"My family situation is...unique."

"You mean with your grandparents?"

She nodded instead of answering.

"I've got it." Noah resettled his hat, looking quite pleased with himself.

"Got what?"

"The solution to my dating disasters."

He leaned forward, close enough that she could smell the shampoo he'd used that morning.

LIEXP0419

"You need to give me dating lessons."

"What do you mean?"

"You and me. We'll go on a few dates…say, three. You can learn how to do anything if you do it three times."

"That's a ridiculous suggestion."

"Why? I learn better from doing."

"Do you?"

"I've already learned not to take a girl to a gas station, but who knows how many more dating traps are waiting for me."

"So this would be…a learning experience."

"It's a perfect solution." He tugged on her *kapp* string, something no one had done to her since she'd been a young teen.

"I can tell by the shock on your face that I've made you uncomfortable. It's a *gut* idea, though. We'd keep it businesslike—nothing personal."

Olivia Mae had no idea why the thought of sitting through three dates with Noah Graber made her stomach twirl like she'd been on a merry-go-round. Maybe she was catching a stomach bug.

"Wait a minute. Are you trying to get out of your third date? Because you promised your *mamm* that you would give this thing three solid attempts."

"And I'll keep my word on that," Noah assured her. "After you've tutored me, you can throw another poor unsuspecting girl my way."

Olivia Mae stood, brushed off the back of her dress and pointed a finger at Noah, who still sat in the grass as if he didn't have a care in the world.

"All right. I'll do it."

Don't miss
A Perfect Amish Match *by Vannetta Chapman,*
available May 2019 wherever
Love Inspired® *books and ebooks are sold.*

www.LoveInspired.com

Inspirational Romance to Warm Your Heart and Soul

Join our social communities to connect with other readers who share your love!

Sign up for the Love Inspired newsletter at **www.LoveInspired.com** to be the first to find out about upcoming titles, special promotions and exclusive content.

CONNECT WITH US AT:

Facebook.com/groups/HarlequinConnection

 Facebook.com/LoveInspiredBooks

 Twitter.com/LoveInspiredBks